"I MUST HAVE MANSOUL AT ANY COST," SAID THE GIANT DIABOLUS. "I WILL SETTLE FOR NOthing less." He was sitting on his haunches, pushing up little mounds of brimstone as he spoke. His war lords sat around him in a circle in one of the private conference caverns of the pit, eyeing the mounds of brimstone. Periodic spurts of fire erupted from crevices and lighted up their faces and sent their shadows shooting up the sides of the walls. From the huge yawning cavern beyond came occasional blasts of hot air, sometimes rushing through the stalactites and stalagmites with a formidable roar, sometimes winding through with great sighs and moans, sometimes in whispers.

# CHRONICLES OF
# Mansoul

---

## A JOHN BUNYAN CLASSIC
## AS TOLD BY
# Ethel Barrett

*cheri nease*

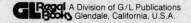 **GL Regal Books** A Division of G/L Publications
Glendale, California, U.S.A.

The foreign language publishing of all Regal books
is under the direction of GLINT.
GLINT provides financial and technical help for the adaptation,
translation and publishing of books in more than 85 languages
for millions of people worldwide.

For more information write:
GLINT, 110 W. Broadway, Glendale, CA 91204.

Published by
Regal Books Division, G/L Publications
Glendale, California 91209
Printed in U.S.A.

Library of Congress Catalog Card No. 75-100980
ISBN 0-8307-0736-0

# CONTENTS

# AUTHOR'S INTRODUCTION

*Chronicles of Mansoul* is written with apologies to John Bunyan, for it is taken from one of his great allegories, *Holy War*. There was a time when I was perfectly sure that nobody but John Bunyan, his printer and I had ever managed to make it all the way through his ponderous classic. I read it long before the days when I had to. I read it, not as a study, but because I was avid for a good story, just for the sheer pleasure of it.

Then I read the scholars. Their consensus was that Bunyan had gone off in too many directions, had tried to encompass too much in too heavy a framework, had interwoven too many themes in one tale. So went the criticism.

But the damage had been done.

I had already read the story and my pristine mind had disregarded all the discursiveness, ignored the counterpoint and weeded out the extraneous, for I was, you see, hungry in my own soul. And I got what I was after. With all this underbrush cut away, I simply got a long hard look at someone I had never really known before.

Me.

Though this allegory was written in the tradition of the popular story and Bunyan's laughter resounded loud and clear in spots, I was nevertheless able to look at myself with a coldly clinical eye, with judgment, and yes, with compassion.

I wanted to be spiritual; I was not. I wanted to be strong; I was not. I wanted to be humble; I was not. I wanted to be all the wonderful things everyone else *seemed* to be. But I was not. I was a bundle of inconsistencies and "born to trouble as the sparks fly upward."

I closed the book, astonished, never to be the same again.

It is in this spirit that I want to present *Chronicles of Mansoul* to you, with all the cobwebs swept away. For it is only when Mansoul is *you* that all the pieces fall into place.

The first three chapters deal with the fall of man. After that, you are, if I may be so vulgar, on your own. For, from there on out, it is an intensely personal story; it is the story of *you*. The inhabitants of Mansoul—all of them—are facets of your own personality—the old man and the new.

Woven through the subtle temptations, the backsliding, the never-ending skirmishes, the pathetic attempts of Mansoul to extricate itself from Satan—is drama and often ironic humor. And shining through the scenes of victory is the glory of God.

As these allegorical characters come to life, the super-strategy and diabolical cunning of Satan is laid bare. In the "dickering" scenes—the court trial—the dramatic quarrel between Mr. Godly-Fear and Mr. Carnal-Security—Bunyan reaches the heights of genius and inspiration.

It is not just a story to read—it is an experience. And when you've read it, you will be filled with wonder—at how little you love God—and how much He loves you . . . .

*Ethel Barrett*

# CAST OF CHARACTERS

### THE MAIN CHARACTERS

King Shaddai, who is God
Prince Emmanuel, who is Christ
The Lord High Secretary,
   who is the Holy Spirit
Diabolus, who is Satan
Mansoul, who is YOU
Lord Mayor Understanding

| | |
|---|---|
| *The chief gentry of Mansoul* | Lord Willbewill (Will)<br>Mr. Conscience<br>Captain Resistance<br>Lord Innocency |

### OTHER CHARACTERS,
in order of appearance

| | |
|---|---|
| *Diabolus' War Lords* | Beelzebub<br>Apollyon<br>Legion<br>Alecto |
| *Diabolus' Aldermen and Constables* | Mr. Haughty<br>Mr. Hard-Heart<br>Mr. Pitiless<br>Mr. Cheating<br>Mr. Incredulity, alias Unbelief |
| *Captains and Standard-Bearers of Shaddai* | Captain Boanerges<br>Mr. Thunder<br>Captain Conviction<br>Mr. Sorrow<br>Captain Judgment<br>Mr. Terror<br>Captain Execution<br>Mr. Justice |

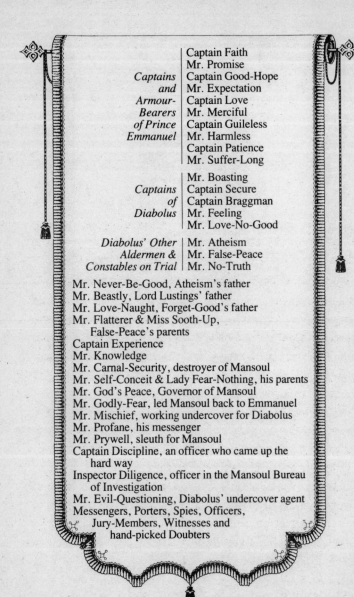

|  |  |
|---|---|
| *Captains and Armour-Bearers of Prince Emmanuel* | Captain Faith<br>Mr. Promise<br>Captain Good-Hope<br>Mr. Expectation<br>Captain Love<br>Mr. Merciful<br>Captain Guileless<br>Mr. Harmless<br>Captain Patience<br>Mr. Suffer-Long |
| *Captains of Diabolus* | Mr. Boasting<br>Captain Secure<br>Captain Braggman<br>Mr. Feeling<br>Mr. Love-No-Good |
| *Diabolus' Other Aldermen & Constables on Trial* | Mr. Atheism<br>Mr. False-Peace<br>Mr. No-Truth |

Mr. Never-Be-Good, Atheism's father

Mr. Beastly, Lord Lustings' father

Mr. Love-Naught, Forget-Good's father

Mr. Flatterer & Miss Sooth-Up,
    False-Peace's parents

Captain Experience

Mr. Knowledge

Mr. Carnal-Security, destroyer of Mansoul

Mr. Self-Conceit & Lady Fear-Nothing, his parents

Mr. God's Peace, Governor of Mansoul

Mr. Godly-Fear, led Mansoul back to Emmanuel

Mr. Mischief, working undercover for Diabolus

Mr. Profane, his messenger

Mr. Prywell, sleuth for Mansoul

Captain Discipline, an officer who came up the
    hard way

Inspector Diligence, officer in the Mansoul Bureau
    of Investigation

Mr. Evil-Questioning, Diabolus' undercover agent

Messengers, Porters, Spies, Officers,
    Jury-Members, Witnesses and
       hand-picked Doubters

# PROLOGUE

NCE UPON A TIME, A LONG, LONG TIME AGO, THERE LIVED A GREAT KING, AND THE NAME OF THIS KING WAS SHADDAI.

NOW SHADDAI HAD BUILT FOR HIMself a great country called Universe, and this country was vast beyond words to describe; it contained enough planets and galaxies of stars to boggle the imagination. As if this were not enough, he had populated it with angels, and over all these angels he had put one angel wiser and more beautiful than all the others, and this angel's name was Lucifer.

Lucifer's task and glory was to carry the government of Shaddai to the angels and to carry back their worship to Shaddai. The situation was perfect. Except for one problem.

The problem was Lucifer.

Lucifer, not content with what he had, wanted to be as powerful as Shaddai himself, and persuaded the angels to rebel, and the place in the Universe where this rebellion was perpetrated was called Earth and Lucifer was confident that the rebellion would be successful.

It was not.

For Shaddai blasted the earth with his judgment and

changed Lucifer's name to Diabolus and banished him and his followers to a miserable pit.

And the story would have ended there, except for one thing.

Shaddai refurbished this place called Earth and on it he built for himself a town and the name of this town was *Mansoul*.

Diabolus snapped to attention.

The story was not over.

The story was just beginning.

For Mansoul was Shaddai's delight. What sweeter revenge could Diabolus have than to take it?

And so we have a great king, a wonderful town that he built for his pleasure, and a wicked giant who hates him. And on these three things hangs a tale of love and intrigue and adventure, a tale of castles and strongholds, of battles and banners and trumpets, of thunder and fire and blood, of princes and lords, or armor shining in the sun—

A tale of life and death.

It all began when Diabolus decided to take Mansoul for himself.

## CONSPIRACY AMID THE BRIMSTONE

MUST HAVE MANSOUL AT ANY COST," SAID THE GIANT DIABOLUS. "I WILL SETTLE FOR NOTHING LESS." HE WAS SITTING ON HIS HAUNCHES, PUSHING UP little mounds of brimstone as he spoke. His war lords sat around him in a circle in one of the private conference caverns of the pit, eyeing the mounds of brimstone. Periodic spurts of fire erupted from crevices and lighted up their faces and sent their shadows shooting up the sides of the walls. From the huge yawning cavern beyond came occasional blasts of hot air, sometimes rushing through the stalactites and stalagmites with a formidable roar, sometimes winding through with great sighs and moans, sometimes in whispers.

"And just how," said one of the war lords, still watching the mounds of brimstone, "do you propose to do this, M'Lord?"

"That is why I called this council, Beelzebub," said Diabolus, looking up for a moment at the speaker. "I do not know exactly how. But of one thing I am sure. It will be easy."

"May I remind you, M'Lord," said Beelzebub, "that this is not B.B."

They all exchanged glances in silence.

1

"B.B.," Beelzebub went on relentlessly—" 'before ban-ishment.' Then you were Lucifer, son of morning, created by the great King Shaddai, ruler over all his angels, carrying his government to the angels, carrying their worship back to him—greatest in beauty, greatest in power—"

"Mansoul is Shaddai's treasure," interrupted Diabolus, beginning to flatten out his mounds of brimstone, "the one creation Shaddai has set his heart on, cares the most about. What sweeter revenge could I possibly have than to take his most precious possession? I must have it."

"You must have it," said Beelzebub. "That is exactly what happened B.B. You were not satisfied with your lot. Your paunch was growling for more. Only that time you cried, 'I will set my throne above the throne of Shaddai. I will *be like* Shaddai.' You wanted nothing less than absolute, ultimate power, and you tried to start a rebellion—"

"I *did* start a rebellion," corrected Diabolus. "And it worked."

"Yes, it worked," said Beelzebub, "if you mean you were successful in getting enough angels to follow you. But it's like saying 'the operation was successful but the patient died.' We were all banished to this miserable pit forever, you and your fallen angels with you."

They were all silent for a moment, watching the mounds of brimstone being pushed up again.

"Because you overlooked one thing," said Beelzebub finally, pressing his point.

"I did not overlook," said Diabolus. "I underesti-mated."

"Underestimated then," said Beelzebub. "The power you sought, King Shaddai had reserved for his son, Prince

2

Emmanuel—in fact had already bestowed upon him.''

"Have you anything more to say?'' said Diabolus.

"And you've had a one-track mind ever since. You hated King Shaddai.''

"And I *hate* King Shaddai. So much that I can think of nothing else. Have you anything more to say?''

"No,'' sighed Beelzebub, "except to repeat, this is A.B.—'after banishment'—and you are living behind the times.''

A long moaning rush of hot air reverberated throughout the huge labyrinth of caverns outside the conference room and expired with a sigh, away off in the distance. They all stopped to listen.

"And stop doodling,'' Beelzebub said at last.

Diabolus swept the mounds of brimstone away in an elaborate gesture and uncrouched himself. "Are you finished?'' he asked Beelzebub.

"I am finished,'' said Beelzebub. "I merely wished to reiterate the facts to be perfectly sure it is clear in our minds what we are up against. Chipping at your arguments to find a possible chink. I am, of course,'' he added, leaning forward hungrily on his haunches, "with you all the way.''

"Of course,'' said Diabolus.

"Provided you are realistic about it.''

"Realistic?''

"You cannot hope ever to become Lord of the Universe.''

"That would be highly improbable.''

"That would be highly impossible.''

"I rather fancy being Lord of the Universe,'' sighed Diabolus, "but one does what one can.''

"You *are* being realistic," said Beelzebub. "What are your plans?"

Diabolus sprang into action. "Apollyon," he said, "hand me that stick, will you? Legion, draw up closer. And Alecto, perhaps you'd better take notes. The rest of you, watch and listen." He leaned forward with the stick Apollyon handed him and began to make marks in the brimstone. "Now," he said, "this whole area is Universe—situated between these two poles—Heaven and Hell. And right— here—is—Mansoul. Here. Now. As you know, Mansoul is a town so fair, so commodious, so wonderful, so—well, it has no equal under Heaven. King Shaddai made it for his delight and for his glory; he gave it dominion over everything around it and it enjoys privileges and powers beyond belief—"

"We know that, we *know* that," said Apollyon. "How are you planning to take this town?"

"There is a wall of course," Diabolus went on, "and five gates. The Ear-gate, the Eye-gate, the Mouth-gate, the Nose-gate, and the Feel-gate. The three highest in power are Lord Mayor Understanding and Lord Willbewill and Mr. Conscience."

"How are you planning to take it?" said Beelzebub.

"How are you planning to take it?" said Apollyon.

Alecto and the others remained silent.

"It's impregnable," Diabolus admitted at last. "The walls are so made that they cannot be scaled or breached without the consent of those inside."

"And the gates?"

"The gates cannot be opened—"

"—without the consent of those inside," they all finished it together.

4

There was a long silence.

"If we muster all our forces—" suggested an underling timidly.

"You are very stupid, my friend," Diabolus shot back. "All our forces would not make a dent. No, my idea—" he paused for effect, "my idea is to make them *want* to let *us* in."

"*Want* to let us in!" they all cried at once. "Who would want to let *us* in?"

"We look pretty seamy, M'Lord," Apollyon finished lamely. "Our onetime princely appearance is a thing of the past."

"I know," said Diabolus. "I'd thought of that. A scrubby lot, all of us, a scrubby lot indeed. One look at us and the whole town would be on a red alert. And that is just my strategy. They will not see us. We will be invisible. And they will not see our intentions either."

"Our intentions will be invisible, too!" said Legion.

"We'll cloak them with lies and deceit!" said Apollyon.

"And flattery!" said Beelzebub.

"Yessss," said Diabolus. "We'll cajole them, delude them, pretending things that will never be and promising things they shall never get. Lies, lies, lies—the only way to get Mansoul to let us in. And so our intentions will be invisible and we will be invisible—that is, all except one of us. And I suggest—" he looked around the circle of faces, "I suggest that I be that one."

"By all means!" they all cried at once. "For you are the genius at deceit, a master liar!"

"*The* master liar," Diabolus corrected. "I say this in all

modesty. There has never been my equal." He waited for someone to challenge him. No one did. "Well then," he said, "now that that's decided, the next question is my disguise. What shall it be?"

They all began to talk at once.

"A mouse! What could be more harmless than a mouse?"

"No! What could be more *stupid* than a mouse?"

"It must be something over which they have dominion!"

"But something they respect!"

"One of those beasts Mansoul deems wiser than the rest!"

"Yes—something wise and beautiful!"

"They must be completely disarmed!"

"What do you think—" said Diabolus, pulling up the threads, "what do you think of something in the dragon family? A dragon answers all those requisites." He waited for their reaction. They sat in silence, thinking of the dragon—slithering along with grace, beautifully colored and shining in the sun. Their eyes narrowed in wicked pleasure.

"Now that that's settled," Diabolus sat up straight and rubbed his hands together. "You—Apollyon—gather your accouterments of warfare, map out your plans, prepare to be within bow-shot of the town with your army. Have your most skilled sharpshooters coached to pick off any leaders of the town who might get in the way. You—Beelzebub. Gather your demons. Appoint a party of handpicked scouts to go before us and keep their eyes and ears open. You—Alecto, send Mr. Ill-Pause to me. I want to use him as my co-speaker in case I should get talked into a corner. And oh, Apolly-on—"

"Yes, M'Lord?"

"Apollyon, there is a certain captain who may give us a bit of trouble. He will undoubtedly be one of those on the city wall. His name is Resistance—Captain Resistance. Have one of your best sharpshooters cover him."

"Yes, M'Lord."

Diabolus turned again to the whole group. "That is all. Council dismissed."

They straggled out of the conference room in small groups, some talking, some whispering, and their voices echoed endlessly through the huge yawning caverns, melding with the roars and sighs and groans and inarticulate whispers.

Diabolus rubbed his hands together as he watched them go. He pictured the great army soon to be amassed, invisible but deadly. He pictured the sharpshooters, bows drawn, awaiting the order to shoot. He pictured his herald sounding the trumpet for an audience. He pictured the gentry of Mansoul climbing up to the top of the wall to listen. And he pictured himself disguised as a beautiful dragon. He hurried off to his own den to get his thoughts together and compose his speech. Of course Mr. Ill-Pause would be on hand to leap in the breach at the slightest hesitation on Mansoul's part. That was his forte. Any conversation that faltered in his presence was doomed. Diabolus was enjoying it already, in fancy. He did hope Mr. Ill-Pause was in fine fettle.

The whole idea was quite heady.

# A SUMMONS TO MANSOUL

ORD MAYOR UNDERSTANDING HAD REACHED THE PEAK OF HIS MORNING WALK. HE ALWAYS CALLED IT THE PEAK, FOR IT WAS THE HIGHEST POINT in the town of Mansoul, the rolling hills on the edge of town, a vantage point from which he could survey all of it—the dwellings nestled in the hills, the meadows awash with flowers, the market square below in the distance, the streets and thoroughfares, the castle in the center, the walls. It all lay, like a picture, before his eyes.

It had been built by the great King Shaddai for his delight and pleasure. He had made it the mirror and glory of all that he was, beyond anything else that he had made in Universe. It was a beautiful place—peaceful and good and strong; there was no other place under the heavens as wonderful as Mansoul.

And as Shaddai had made it beautiful, so he had also made it powerful. Indeed the town of Mansoul had dominion over all the country round about. All were commanded to do homage to it. The town itself had positive commission and power from King Shaddai to demand service of all, and to subdue any that denied it.

It was a glorious day, like all the other days before and like all the days ahead promised to be. Lord Understanding paused there, as he always did, and looked and marveled that each day could be so filled with endless new things, with such a variety of joys. There was no lack, no sorrow, no pain, no rascals, no sin. There was enough of everything and everything was good. And there was only one law: to love King Shaddai and to do his will, and his will was perfect and a delight to do.

Lord Mayor Understanding started back toward the castle to begin his day's work. He felt the same thrill he felt every morning: the thrill of descending into this picture of perfect beauty and becoming a living part of it.

Then the shrill sound of a trumpet shattered the air and shattered his thoughts.

He stopped and listened. The air was clear and silent for a moment. Then the trumpet sounded again, and this time the notes hung in the air, demanding, beguiling, beckoning.

A summons? It sounded like a summons. He could not be sure. But of this he was sure; it was strange and exotic, unlike anything he had ever heard before. He forgot his leisurely morning walk, and pummeled through the tangled foliage until he was on the streets again. Then he ran at breakneck speed down into the center of town, then across it, toward the city walls.

Back in the castle, Mr. Conscience was sitting at his desk, facing a large expanse of windows that commanded a magnificent view of the castle gardens, the castle walls, and much of the town beyond. He never tired of this view. He never tired of the castle. It was reared up in the very middle of the town, a most stately palace. For strength it might be called a

9

castle; for pleasantness, a paradise; for largeness, a place so copious as to seem to contain, in miniature, the very Universe itself. This was the heart, the core, the innermost being of Mansoul. This was the place King Shaddai intended for himself alone; partly because of his own delights and partly because he did not want the tyranny of strangers upon the town. And this was the secret place. Shaddai came here in the cool of the day, to enjoy Mansoul. Here he would visit with both the gentry and the townspeople, and their fellowship was sweet beyond words to tell.

Things were beginning to stir. Mr. Conscience could hear Captain Resistance in the next room, giving orders to his staff. The market square was beginning to fill up with the people of Mansoul; the shops were opening and folk were coming out of their houses. Mr. Conscience could see the great seal of Shaddai in the distance, commanding the square. He thought of the other seal of Shaddai on the outside of the castle gates, and of Shaddai's banners unfurled on the topmost towers of the castle, whipping and snapping in the morning breeze. He never tired of the sight; he always stopped and gazed at it in love and gratitude before he started his morning walk. He shifted the papers on his desk and then got up and stretched. Perhaps Captain Resistance might join him in his walk this morning; they had much to talk about. Resistance held a position of great responsibility but he was a strong man and capable, always ready to stand by his convictions. It was always good to talk to him. Conscience was halfway to the door when he heard it.

The sound of a trumpet. It filled the air and seemed to stay there, demanding, commanding. A summons? From whom? And why? Mr. Conscience froze in his tracks. There it was

10

again. It *was* a summons. He tore out the door, down the corridor, down the stairs, through the spacious halls and foyer downstairs, out the castle door. He was halfway down the castle steps when he thought of Captain Resistance. He stopped, started back, just as Resistance bolted out of the castle door. Without a word they ran to the castle gates and out into the street.

The trumpet was sounding again. They made for the city wall.


Lord Willbewill was making his morning rounds. Every morning he walked all the way around the walls of Mansoul, inspecting them and delighting in their beauty. They were built for strength too; so fast and firm were they structured, that had it not been for the townsmen themselves, they could not have been shaken or broken forever. For here lay the excellent wisdom of Shaddai, that the walls could never be breached nor harmed by the mightiest adversary or potentate unless the townsmen gave consent. Willbewill had five gates to inspect: Ear-gate, Eye-gate, Mouth-gate, Nose-gate, and Feel-gate. These were also impregnable; they could never be opened nor forced unless the Mansoulians gave consent. Mansoul could never perish, except from within. As he walked along he thought of his relationship with Shaddai. It was a very wonderful and mysterious thing. Shaddai loved him, that he knew; how great that love was he could not fathom. The wonder of it was that Shaddai loved him; the mystery of it was that Shaddai did not command his love in return, but left him free, left him with the awesome power of choice.

11

Was that, then, the mystery of love—to be chosen, to have the power to choose? He exulted in the thought. At this moment he did not know that the power of choice made love both the most powerful and the most fragile of all relationships. Nor did he know that while he was exulting over its greatest strength he was in danger of stumbling over its greatest weakness.

The shattering sound of the trumpet almost sent him sprawling.

He staggered and would have fallen had he not flailed out at the wall for support. It blasted through him and sent his head spinning; he leaned against the wall, shaken. There it was again, deafening, commanding. A summons? Ear-gate was just ahead. He ran toward it and in his confusion he thought he saw a figure climbing up the steps to the wall. Almost in the same moment he realized that the figure was real. It was Lord Innocency.

His head cleared. It was a summons all right. He headed for the steps and began to climb them, and halfway up he turned and looked over the streets of Mansoul. The people had stopped in their tracks, listening. Then he saw in the distance Mr. Conscience and Captain Resistance running toward the gate. He stopped, decided to wait for them. Lord Mayor Understanding was somewhere out for his morning walk. He must have heard the summons too. They would all wait for him, thought Willbewill. It would be proper for them to all appear together. He called out to Lord Innocency to wait. Then he sat down on the steps. He wished that it were the cool of the day and that Shaddai were here. But the wish was only for a moment.

He was free to make his own choices.

## THE FIRST ASSAULT

ORD INNOCENCY WAS THE FIRST TO LOOK OVER THE CITY WALL, AND ALL HE SAW WAS A DRAGON. "OH," HE THOUGHT, "WHAT BEAUTIFUL COLORS!"

Lord Willbewill was right behind him, and then Lord Mayor Understanding and Mr. Conscience, and last of all, Captain Resistance.

Down in the fields below, Diabolus' invisible army was camped, waiting.

"Pssst," whispered Apollyon to his sharpshooter, "that's Captain Resistance on the end. Don't take your eyes off him." And he thought to himself, "He's going to give old Diabolus some trouble; I can tell by his stance. Stiff as a ramrod." He shifted his position so he could study them better, causing nothing more than a small rustle in the grass. What a sorry lot they were, he thought scornfully, Lord Innocency, dewy-eyed and fresh as the morning. And Mr. Conscience, the town recorder. And what did he have to record? There was no law except to love Shaddai. And Lord Mayor Understanding. Ah now, there was one to envy;

13

Shaddai had given him the power to perceive, to comprehend, to discern. He would be a dangerous one indeed, left to himself. Old Diabolus would not have a chance.

But, Apollyon wondered, why had Shaddai, in creating for himself this glorious town, done that one incomprehensible thing? He had left himself vulnerable by installing Mr. Willbewill in the town, yea, as one of the very gentry of Mansoul. And he had given Willbewill the power to make choices. Now the ramifications of this were enough to stagger the imagination. How Shaddai could have put himself in such a hazardous position was an unfathomable mystery. Why create a creature for one's glory and delight, and then give that creature the power and the prerogative to deny one? Why not make it impossible for the creature to have any power of choice? Ah, but then it would not be love. For the greatest thing about love is to be chosen.

Willbewill was shouting something from the wall.

But what a chance for Shaddai to take, Apollyon concluded, as he stirred himself and got into position. What a precarious gamble! If one did not hate Shaddai one could almost pity him for putting himself in a position to be rejected by his most beloved creation.

"Who are you?" Willbewill was shouting. "And what do you want?" Apollyon looked over at his sharpshooter, who had stiffened to attention.

"Why did you come?" Willbewill was shouting. "State your mission, please." Everyone in Diabolus' great army waited, paunches growling, hungry for the prey, and every eye was on the old master and his colleague Ill-Pause.

And, like a lamb, Diabolus began his carefully prepared speech. "I am not a stranger," he said. His voice was oily. "I

14

am, in fact, a neighbor. It is my duty to the great King Shaddai to drop by and pay you my respects and offer you my services. It is also my pleasure.'' He bowed low. ''I am your humble servant, seeking only your welfare, and, quite frankly, it is not my advantage, but yours I seek—it is because of my great concern for you that I have come.''

''Concern? For us? Our welfare?'' Lord Mayor Understanding spoke up. His voice was polite but remote.

''Clearly you do not understand what I mean,'' said Diabolus with carefully feigned patience. ''And no wonder. For the laws of your king are so intricate.''

''But we have but one law—to love Shaddai and to do his will.''

''Ah, that is just it. That is what it *seems* like. But your king—don't misunderstand me! I do not deny his greatness but his law is nonetheless intricate. First he says you may eat of all of the fruit of the garden and then he forbids you to eat the fruit of one tree. So you see, though you ostensibly have freedom, you are actually in bondage. To get down to cases, I have come to show you how to obtain deliverance from this bondage you are in. Surely you cannot object to that.''

Apollyon's sharpshooter prepared to draw his bow. ''Not—yet, not yet,'' hissed Apollyon. He did not take his eyes off Resistance. ''Be ready. I'll tell you.''

''Bondage? But we were not aware that we were in bondage!'' They all spoke at once. Their amazement was written on their faces.

Diabolus followed his advantage quickly. ''That's just it. You were not *aware*. You are not aware of what you are missing.''

Captain Resistance narrowed his eyes and stared at

Diabolus. Apollyon gestured again for the sharpshooter to stay his hand.

"Now?" asked the sharpshooter, a moment later.

"Not yet, not yet," cautioned Apollyon.

"Your king has forbidden you to eat the fruit of the tree of knowledge of good and evil. Right?" said Diabolus. They nodded. "Do you not have a right to that knowledge?" he went on, and then answered his own question. "Certainly you do. The one thing he has forbidden you to have is the very thing that will do you the most good. How can you be complete without it? You must have knowledge and understanding."

They stared at each other, then back at him. Apollyon and his sharpshooter waited.

"He tells you," Diabolus was speaking quickly now, "he tells you if you eat that fruit you will die. That is not—quite true. Your eyes will be opened, and you shall be as gods!"

The grass stirred and rustled impatiently under the shifting of the invisible army.

"So I repeat," said Diabolus, "his laws are intricate and rather unfair. You are in bondage."

Captain Resistance stiffened.

The sharpshooter drew his bow and took careful aim. "Now?" he said.

"Yes—before he speaks. Now! Let him have it!" Apollyon hissed.

A gleaming arrow shot through the air and found its mark. Captain Resistance tottered a few steps forward. He hesitated a moment, then pitched over the wall—quite dead.

The officials of Mansoul were horrified. The town was

16

now without courage or heart to resist. Mr. Conscience looked completely bewildered. Lord Willbewill stared at Diabolus with new eyes. Lord Mayor Understanding looked as if someone had dealt him a blow. And while they stood thus, Mr. Ill-Pause stepped forward. This was just what he was waiting for. The first bit of uncertainty, the first hesitation.

"Gentlemen, *gentlemen*," he cried.

They stared at him. In the shock of Captain Resistance's death they had not seen him appear; they concluded that they just had not noticed him before.

"Gentlemen," he said softly now that he had their attention. "What my master says is true. We can only hope that you will be reasonable and accept his advice. He has a very great love for you. And though he well knows he runs the risk of King Shaddai's anger, his love for you is such that he is willing to take that risk. I have only this to add. I beg you to consider his words. Remember that you have no power—"

They looked at each other. No power?

"—that you know very little—"

They looked back at him.

"—and that this is the way to know more. If you do not accept this good counsel—" he shook his head sadly—"then you are not the men I took you to be."

There was a long silence. Only the rustling of the grass. And then finally—

"Ah," said Lord Mayor Understanding. "it *would* be nice to have all knowledge and understan—" He suddenly noticed that Innocency was beginning to tremble.

"M'Lord Innocency, is something the matter?"

Innocency began to sway and wobble where he stood.

"—all knowledge and—M'Lord, you look pale. What is the matter?"

Innocency's knees were buckling.

"M'Lord, if you are ill—oh! M'Lord Willbewill! Mr. Conscience!"

Innocency sank quietly where he was, and sprawled flat, apparently lifeless. The officials gathered around and bent over him, slapping his wrists. Lord Mayor Understanding stood there shocked and waiting. After a long moment, Willbewill straightened up.

"He's dead, M'Lord Mayor. Sinking spell, it would seem. Took him suddenly."

"Ah," said Lord Mayor Understanding, "that is sad."

And sad it was, indeed. For Innocency and Resistance were the beauty and glory of Mansoul—the two opponents Diabolus feared the most. The others stood there, shocked, waiting. Then—

"It will not hurt to consider what the dragon says," said Lord Mayor Understanding. He looked at Lord Willbewill.

"Let's go call a meeting," said Willbewill.

And that is exactly what they did. First they went to have a look at the forbidden fruit. Then they considered the idea. Then they fell to, and began to eat.

As the moments flew by, Diabolus and his army waited outside, every eye on the gates. Then finally . . . .

"The Ear-gate! It's opening!"

The cry went up like thunder and it seemed to fill the Universe and reach the heavens and rumble along the plains and echo through the pit in the distance.

And even as they watched, the Eye-gate opened, too.

The rustling grass seemed to shiver though the sun was

18

shining and the plain was warm, and then it was suddenly alive with thousands of demons and war lords of every rank, all with their accouterments of warfare. Diabolus and his great army materialized as if out of thin air. They broke ranks and rushed forward; it was hard to hold them back.

"Wait!"

It was the old master, Diabolus. They came to a reluctant halt.

"Swarm if you must," he said, "but swarm in quietly. I want no nonsense. Do nothing to alarm them. And do not destroy anything—yet. I have other plans. Ready? F'ward—MARCH!"

And in they marched and the gates closed behind them.

It was amazing, how simple it was after all, Apollyon thought as he was swept along with the crowds. What fools these town officials were. They had not only let Diabolus in with all his horde, but had welcomed him warmly. Innocency was dead. Captain Resistance was dead. Mansoul had been given free will to choose in the person of Lord Willbewill. What a monstrously extravagant demonstration of love, Apollyon pondered, to trust something one wanted to keep enough to give it the prerogative to choose to leave. And now the moment had come and the choice had been made. Shaddai had loved; Shaddai had lost. Shaddai was already forgotten.

Diabolus was way up ahead, leading the parade, flanked by the officials and gentry of Mansoul. They marched right up the main street, through the middle of town and into the market square. It was there that Diabolus faced the people of

Mansoul who had gathered to see the one they thought was their deliverer.

"Alas! My poor Mansoul!" he cried amidst the cheering; then waited for it to die down. "I have done you this great service—not for any gain of mine, but because of my great concern for you. I have set you at liberty—"

The cheering was overwhelming; Diabolus signaled for quiet.

"—But alas, I have also left you without a ruler—someone to defend you."

There was a rumble of dismay.

Diabolus followed his advantage quickly, "For when King Shaddai hears of your rebellion, he will come storming in to snatch away that liberty—"

The noise increased.

"Now if I *were* to become your ruler in order to protect you—"

Sure enough

"I accept!" he cried with feigned modesty as he was swept upon shoulders and borne aloft for all to see. It was as simple as that. They swallowed this bramble without even gagging; Diabolus became the king of Mansoul.

Mansoul had fallen. Mansoul was lost.

# ANOTHER ADMINISTRATION

HE FIRST THING DIABOLUS DID WAS THE OBVIOUS THING TO DO. HE TOOK POSSESSION OF THE BEAUTIFUL CASTLE IN THE CENTER OF MANSOUL AND MADE IT his den—his headquarters, he would have corrected quickly. He garrisoned his war lords and more important soldiers within its high walls and forts; he strengthened and fortified it with all sorts of provisions against emergency. Soldiers of lesser importance scurried about the side streets and back streets and found homes for themselves and their families.

Mansoul was not the same. The streets, the lovely avenues, the market square, the places of communion and the places for decision-making—all were cluttered with Diabolus' soldiers. But in spite of all of this, he still did not feel secure.

"Aren't you satisfied?" said his war lords. "You accomplished the skullduggery—eh—task you started out to do."

"Accomplished?" said Diabolus. "I have not even begun." And he called a high-echelon meeting to discuss ways and means of furthering his purposes. The culprits gathered in the beautiful conference room of the castle and slouched around the conference table, their faces reflected in the highly polished surface. Diabolus took charge quickly.

"The first thing we must do, my dear muckworms," he said, "is to remodel. And what does one do when one remodels? One sets up one thing and pulls down another, at pleasure."

They all agreed. Each one had ideas of his own of how this should be done.

"Some officials in Mansoul are up and obviously must come down," he said. "And some are down and must go up. So. We are going to remodel."

They began to squirm and mumble, gleefully.

"Quiet!" said Diabolus. "I know you have pet projects, my scrubby upstarts—but first things first. And one thing at a time. The first remodeling job is the mayor—his excellency, Lord Mayor Understanding." He eyed them with a cold stare until they were quiet. Then he muttered to himself, "Blueprints, blueprints, where'd I put those blueprints— oh—yes, here they are," and he fumbled about and at last held them aloft.

"Now. I submit these plans for a tower to be erected on the site indicated." And he spread the plans out for all to see.

"It's right outside his palace windows," said Alecto.

"Between his palace windows—" said Beelzebub.

"And the sun," Diabolus finished. "Make his palace nice and dark. D'you see?"

"But he's friendly to us. He complied with the rest of the town gentry in letting us in," they all said at once.

22

"Yes, I know," said Diabolus, not looking up from the blueprint. "He is also a very understanding man. He sees too much. That is something you seem to have overlooked, my snakes-in-the-grass. He cannot be allowed to live in his former luster and glory."

He straightened up. "By limited liberties, by living in darkness, he will be useful to us and a hindrance to Mansoul. We can depend on him to confuse and distort—"

"But they can't be any more confused than they are already—"

"Oh yes they can," said the old master. "A darkened understanding has limitless possibilities. By being deprived of light he can become as one born blind. And by being kept a prisoner—"

"You intend to go that far?" they said.

"Certainly, I intend to go that far."

"Will you get away with it?"

"He will be allowed to go out on parole occasionally, but only within his own bounds—no farther. And I shall set those bounds. Of course I'll get away with it. With Understanding darkened and shackled, what can the rest of Mansoul do? Now. Next I would like—"

A deafening roar reverberated through the castle and the windows rattled and the drapes swayed, and the golden dishes and goblets danced on the sideboards, and the dust bunnies that had accumulated since the invasion scurried across the room and caught on the fringe of the priceless rugs and tapestries, and the blueprints took off from the table with a swish, like paper airplanes sent on errant flights.

"Burn my brimstone," muttered Diabolus, "he's at it again. That roar is coming from the house of Mr. Conscience.

And that, my cronies, is just what I was coming to—my next project. Mr. Conscience. He was partly responsible for letting us in—true, true—*Come out from under the table!''*

They came crawling out from whence they had dived, and slithered back onto their respective chairs, a bit sheepishly.

Diabolus looked at them with solicitude. ''You are handpicked whelps and mongrels, tried and false,'' he said softly. ''Are you afraid of a little tantrum of poor old Mr. Conscience?''

Their faces said plainly that they were.

''Where was I,'' said Diabolus, ignoring both the noise and their reaction to it. ''Oh yes. It is not in my power to do *away* with Mr. Conscience. We must, unfortunately, put up with him.''

''But when he roars, sire? What'll we do when he roars?'' said Alecto. ''This is terrible. I'm secretary of this council and I can't even take notes, the table is shaking so.''

''You will take notes of our treachery as best you can,'' said Diabolus. ''And the rest of you rogues will pay attention. We must get a campaign underway—''

''But you cannot dispose of Mr. Conscience the way you can Lord Understanding!'' they cried.

''True. But we can render him impotent.''

''Not entirely!''

''True. But we can make him look like a fool when he *does* cry out.''

''But we can never—''

''Listen to me,'' Diabolus said. He now measured his words and spoke with such conviction that for a moment they were quiet. ''With the proper tactics we can deal the one most devastating blow possible; we can make him look ridiculous.

24

Hear me. First, we debauch him. We lead him into sin. Then we harden his heart with vanity. We keep him so deluded that when he is merry he will do the very things he bellows against. We spread the rumor that he is subject to fits. When he *is* stricken with thoughts of King Shaddai and raises his voice like thunder it will be easy to convince the townspeople that it is one of his bad days. When he tries more mild reasoning we will convince them that he is just prattling.''

''But sire—''

''And when he gets too troublesome, we lull him to sleep so he will stay in a stupor for weeks at a time.''

''Master, M'Lord—''

''Quiet. When we get finished the people of Mansoul will take whatever Mr. Conscience has to say with their tongues in their cheeks. He will bother no one.''

They were all silent for a full moment.

Then, ''But Mr. Conscience will never be wholly yours,'' they said at last.

Diabolus' eyes were like fire. ''Perhaps not. But we can convince them that he is quite mad.'' He walked over to a window and looked out toward the house of Mr. Conscience. ''No,'' he said, ''he will never be wholly ours.''

They adjourned the meeting then, and shuffled out dejectedly, their spirits quite dampened.

But not for long.

They lost no time in getting thse projects started. First the tower was built to keep Lord Understanding in darkness, and guards were posted so that he had to stay within bounds. All propaganda getting in to him was carefully gone over and thoroughly mixed up and confused so that he was quite helpless.

25

And as Diabolus' campaign flourished, poor Mr. Conscience was despised and neglected by the people of Mansoul. If, at odd times, he did disturb them, Diabolus would run to the rescue and make this his subject in one of his deceptively chatty talks to the town. "Hush, my Mansoul," he would croon, "are you not more content than you ever were before? You know you are! Consider how I have served you, even to the full extent of my power, and given you the very best that I have, or could procure for you in all the world. Your liberty has been enlarged by me. I found you shackled and I set you free. You have no laws. I do not hold you to account for your doings. I have let you live-and-let-live with as little control from me as I have from you. What more do you want? There, there, *there* now. That's better. And don't let that horrid rumbling disturb you.

"It is just twaddle," he would go on, warming to his subject, "that's all it is. And with all Mr. Conscience's high talk, you hear nothing of Shaddai himself, now do you? *Do* you?"

He would wait dramatically for the answer that never came.

"Well!" he would say at the end, as if that settled everything. And then he would think to himself, "There. *That* should hold them for a while."

But he never did believe it. For he knew that every outcry of Mr. Conscience against the sin of Mansoul was the voice of God in him to them. Mr. Conscience was clearly the one creature Diabolus feared most of all in Mansoul.

Now, as Diabolus had said, all the remodeling wasn't tearing down. Indeed, some of the changes that did him the most good were the officials he put *in* power. And of all officials to put into power, Lord Willbewill was the most important. He had, to begin with, privileges peculiar to himself in the town of Mansoul. And together with these he was a man of great strength, resolution and courage.

Diabolus was thinking of these attributes as he waited for Willbewill to show up at the castle for an appointment one evening. Strength, resolution and courage. Well actually, thought Diabolus, Willbewill was headstrong—proud and willful was what he was; he was a good man to have on your side. Play on his pride, that's it. Make him one of the great ones. He's the greatest deterrent to Mr. Conscience you can possibly have. Old Conscience cannot be annihilated, no. But he can be militated against, yes. And Willbewill is the man for the job.

"Eh?" said Diabolus aloud, looking up. Willbewill was standing before him.

"I took the liberty of ushering him in," said an underling.

"You were talking to yourself," said Willbewill. "Something about 'man for the job.' "

"Eh—yes. Yes. Sit down, M'Lord," said Diabolus.

"Business. Always business," said Willbewill pleasantly.

Idiot, thought Diabolus. He's going to be garrulous as usual. Can I get nothing done without talking trivia? But aloud he said, "Yesss—always business. Matter of fact I *was* thinking 'man for the job'—and I was thinking of you."

"Of me?" said Willbewill.

Good grief, thought Diabolus, does he have to repeat everything I say? He pushed a box of cigars forward and rustled some papers on his desk to compose himself.

"I sent for you," he said at last, "because you were one

27

of the first chumps to be hoodwinked—eh—the first luminary to accept my counsel and advise opening Ear-gate and letting me in, and you have seemed willing to serve me since my reign began here. Also you are a very stubborn headstrong man and I have a great affection for you.''

"Oh, thank you, sire,'' said Willbewill. "May I speak freely?''

"Oh yesyesyesyesyesyesyes. Go ahead.''

"I have always been a man of considerable importance in this town." Willbewill cleared his throat. "I—if I do say so myself—I am a man capable of making decisions.''

"Ah yes,'' said Diabolus, looking back innocently.

"I—well quite frankly I will not be put in a subordinate position.''

"No, of course.'' Diabolus' innocent stare remained intact.

"I think I rate a position of authority.''

Diabolus almost laughed aloud, but he controlled himself. "A position of authority,'' he said, almost too heartily. Now *he* was repeating. "But of course. That is *exactly* what I was thinking when you came in.''

"You were?'' said Willbewill, delighted.

I said I was, thought Diabolus. Why does he keep repeating? We go around in circles. "I was.'' "You were?'' "I was.'' What a dreary bore. Aloud he said, "I was.''

"To be sure,'' said Willbewill.

Diabolus got up and walked over to stare out of the window. With this kind of a fool in power, he thought, there is no limit to the heights I can reach. Underneath his lofty exterior lies the soul of a string-saver. He turned to face Willbewill. "I'll give you a responsible position. I'll make you captain of the castle—governor of the wall—eh—keeper of the gates—"

Willbewill started to speak but Diabolus put his hand up to indicate that he was not finished. "We'll put a clause in your contract that nothing in the town of Mansoul can be done without your consent. How do you like that?"

Willbewill nodded to indicate that he did.

"And we'll give you a secretary," Diabolus went on. "I already have a man lined up for the job. Fellow by the name of Mr. Mind. Just imagine, the whole town will have to kowtow to the whims of Will and Mind, how do you like *that?*"

Diabolus did not wait for an answer. He rushed on. "You can be the big boss—under my—eh, supervision, of course. You'll be the biggest yes-man—eh, fool—eh, *statesman*. Statesman is the word I want. The biggest statesman Mansoul has ever known."

"Oh *thank* you, sire," sighed Willbewill.

"My pleasure," said Diabolus. "Of course you will take an oath of fidelity to me. Just a matter of form."

"Oh yes, of course, sire."

"And Mr. Conscience—"

"Oh I understand about him, sire." And Willbewill made a circle with his index finger, pointing to his head.

"Exactly," said Diabolus, making a similar gesture. "It would be better if you did not even talk to him. Oh. And when you and Mr. Mind get your offices ready and clean out the old files—if there *should* be any old parchments hanging about, would you—?"

"Of course," said Willbewill. "All old contracts, laws, pledges and fidelities shall be thrown out."

"We understand each other," said Diabolus gravely, and stood to indicate that the interview was over.

"Thank you for giving me this appointment," said Willbewill. "It is good to know that I shall still be my own master. After all, a person of my standing—"

"Of course," said Diabolus.

Willbewill whirled about, went to the door, opened it and turned. "I am the master of my fate—" he blustered.

"Yes."

"I am the captain of my soul!"

"Yes."

The door closed.

"You are a fool," said Diabolus softly. "There is no bigger fool than Will with a whip in his hand." A gust of wind came through the window and blew out the candle and left him there in the darkness, his red eyes glowing.

As the days went on, it became apparent that the success of Diabolus' strategy depended upon his choice of officials.

Diabolus was very scrupulous about this. Inasmuch as Mansoul was the most ancient of corporations before he came to it, he feared that if he did not maintain greatness they might object that he had done them an injury. And so that they might see that he did not intend to lessen their grandeur or to take from them any of their advantageous things, he carefully chose officers who would content them as well as please him.

Some changes were necessary, of course. It took a bit of legerdemain. His excellency, Lord Mayor Understanding, for instance. Inasmuch as he was temporarily disabled, it became necessary to appoint a new mayor. And Lord Lustings was just the man for the job. His platform was "I want what I want when I want it." And as he had no eyes or ears, he could be depended upon to fall in line.

And then of course a new town recorder was necessary, with poor Mr. Conscience completely unfit for his job, and completely unable to keep his nose out of the affairs of Mansoul. The man appointed had to be able to cope with this. He was. His name was Forget-Good; he could remember nothing but mischief and do it with a delight. He was just naturally prone to do things that were hurtful. He kept Mr. Conscience in a coma most of the time.

"Ah yes," said Diabolus. "When those who sit aloft are corrupt themselves, they corrupt the whole region and country where they are." He was sitting at his desk in the castle, going over some official papers.

"Put the right men in power," he said, "and everything else takes care of itself. What have we here? Ah yes. The list of new aldermen and constables. Mmm. Fine. Mr. Haughty, Mr. Hard-Heart, Mr. Pitiless, Mr. Cheating, Mr. Incredulity—who is he? Oh yes. He's the fellow they call Unbelief. Surly chap—he'll do very well. And Mr. False-Peace. He's a good one. Mr. Atheism, I've always fancied him. Yessss. These'll do fine. And the bailiffs and sergeants—oh fine. They're all relatives of the aldermen. I guess I can okay this." He scribbled his signature across it.

Then he reached across his desk toward his box of brim-stone cigars. Yes. Put the right men in power and everything else falls in place. With these officials installed, things would undoubtedly go comfortably from bad to worse.

HINGS DID GO COMFORTABLY FROM BAD TO WORSE, RUNNING MORE OR LESS ON THEIR OWN MOMENTUM NOW THAT DIABOLUS HAD SET UP THE machinery. After he had satisfied himself that only the officials who would serve his ends were in power, he was free to turn his mind to other projects. His hours in his office were full; there was no end of things to do. Mopping-up operations! Officials and underlings streamed through his office endlessly.

"Master?"

"Yes, yes?"

"Mr. No-Truth to see you."

"Oh yes. I sent for him. Have him come in." And he would chortle and check his cigar box and seat his guest and rub his hands and talk, talk, talk, if the guest were a Mansoulian. But he would get right down to business if the guest were one of his own.

"Mr. No-Truth, there's a seal on the castle gates."

"Yes, sire, the seal of Shadd—"

"Never mind that. You know I cannot bear the mention of his name."

"I'm sorry, sire."

"Anyhow this seal of—it makes me nervous."

"I understand."

"You understand? I didn't call you here to take up my time with sympathy. Do something about it."

"What would you have me do, sire?"

"Deface it, distort it, dismantle it."

"My pleasure, sire. I'll do it at once."

"Besides, it is more fitting that my seal be put up there."

"Of course, sire. I was just about to mention it."

"And, No-Truth?"

"Yes, sire?"

"There's another seal of—just like it, down in the market square. Could you take care of that one, too?"

"My pleasure."

And so things went. Symbols, seals, laws and statutes were either destroyed, twisted or touched up, to suit the new government. But the work was never done.

For it is one thing to take a town and quite another thing to keep it.

Some of the projects were on a more gigantic scale. Diabolus would chortle and fuss and argue in turn with his engineers, wanting to know every detail.

"Are these the latest blueprints?"

"Yes, sire."

"This fort is to be built next to the Eye-gate. A most strategic spot, both to command the town, and to keep light from getting in. I'm going to call it the 'Hold of Defiance.' Good name, eh?"

"Oh yes, sire."

"And I'm going to commission Mr. Spite-God to command it. He'll watch over it with diligence, I'm sure. Good man.''

There were other forts. And Diabolus was happy. He hummed and bustled and gawked, sidewalk superintending while they were being built. One could find him almost any afternoon snooping about one or another. There was Midnight Hold, built next to the castle of the ex-mayor, Lord Understanding, to keep Mansoulians from discovering what fools they were. When it was finished and a commander was needed, Mr. Love-No-Light was just the man for the job. And there was Diabolus' favorite, built right in the market square for all to see. He called it Sweet-sin Hold and commissioned Mr. Love-Flesh to command it.

That was the last major project for the present, and after it was finished, Diabolus went back to his castle to muse over what he had done and to gloat. Indeed, he had plenty to gloat over. He had taken Mansoul, lock, stock and barrel, settled himself and his army within, put down old officers, set up new ones, defaced the great seal of Shaddai, set up his own, spoiled old law books, promoted his own lies, made new magistrates, set up new aldermen, built new forts and manned them—

''Why it's practically foolproof,'' he said. ''I haven't left a loophole. Not one!'' Whereupon he crouched uncomfortably in one of his favorite positions and dreamed him a dream of power and more power—

And that's the way he was when the awful news reached him.


What Diabolus hadn't known was that, even as the Ear-gate of Mansoul was being thrown open on that fateful day, a messenger was on his way to the far country of the great King Shaddai to tell him that Mansoul had fallen, in fact had delivered itself into enemy hands. And that evening as Diabolus was poring over plans for remodeling, that same messenger was standing before the great king and his son in open court, with all the high lords, captains and nobles there to hear. The messenger's report was faithful in announcing, that—

ITEM! Diabolus had come upon Mansoul with craft, blandishments, subtlety, lies and guile, and ITEM! he had treacherously slain the right noble Captain Resistance as he stood upon the wall and ITEM! that Lord Innocency had fallen down dead with a sinking spell, some say with grief, and ITEM! that varlet Ill-Pause had made a short oration to the townsmen in behalf of his master Diabolus, and ITEM! the simple town, believing that what was said was true, had with one consent opened Ear-gate and let the vandals in, and ITEM! Diabolus had stripped Lord Mayor Understanding and Mr. Conscience, the town recorder, of all their powers and all their rights and, ITEM! Lord Willbewill had turned traitor and pledged allegiance to the renegade giant and was granted great powers that he was using to do mischief, and ITEM! the new mayor and recorder were Lord Lustings and Mr. Forget-Good, and ITEM! Diabolus had built several strong towers, forts and strongholds to fortify Mansoul against Shaddai's influence, and ITEM! the list of aldermen and burgesses was scandalous—and so on and on, all of it.

And the bad news, well, it jolted Diabolus right out of his favorite position.

"What did you say?" he asked one of his intelligence officers as he was uncrouching himself.

"The account of all your doings was delivered in open court," said the briefing officer, "the king and his son, Emmanuel, and the high lords and chief captains and nobles were all present."

"Yes, yes, yes, yes, yes, I know all that."

"There was sorrow and grief to think that Mansoul was lost."

"Yes, yes, the other—get to the other."

"King Shaddai and his son, Prince Emmanuel, foresaw all this when they first made the Universe."

"Yes, get on, get on."

"They planned that at an affixed time, Prince Emmanuel would pay for Mansoul's rebellion by his own death."

"And?"

"That Shaddai would raise him from the dead."

"Sssssssssssssss." Diabolus let out a long sibilant sound like that of a goose, and rocked his head back and forth in his hands. Then there was a long silence. Finally he said, "Go on. We may as well have it all."

"It has already been done. Mansoul is redeemed. Bought. Paid for."

"That's what I thought you said," Diabolus said wearily, "but I didn't believe it. Now. Have you repeated everything? Is there more?"

"There is more."

Diabolus' eyes grew bright like burning coals, stirred up and glowing. "Say on."

"They have drawn up a record, telling of all these things," said the intelligence officer quickly, backing away. "Under the supervision of the Lord High Secretary in Shaddai's court. It's to be published. It's called the word of Shaddai. The Bible. and that's not all."

"All, then, all. The rest of it, quickly!"

"Emmanuel intends to make war on you, even now while you're still here, and take the town of Mansoul back, and live in it!"

Diabolus flew into action. He pressed desk buzzers and pulled bell cords and had his staff getting stuck in doorways attempting to carry out his orders.

"Where's Apollyon?"

"He was going on liberty, sire. He—"

"Cancel it."

"But Beelzebub was to cover for him, sire, and—"

"Cancel it. Cancel all liberties."

"Yes, sire."

"Our enemy slumbers not; neither shall we."

"No, sire."

"Put all my war lords on alert; they're to stand by, on call."

"Yes, sire."

And all through the forenoon, Diabolus' voice rang through the castle—"Get some posters printed giving the townspeople new liberties—permission to do as they please, the worse the better.

"Let down the censorship. Anything goes, in literature, in songs, in plays—everything, anything. That'll keep them busy for a while. Ought to weaken them too. And perhaps it will convince Prince Emmanuel that they're not worth saving.

"Somebody get in touch with Mr. Forget-Good. I want Conscience to have a sleeping pill.

"Call for a new vote of confidence. We'll have parades and music and speeches and get them all whipped up, and then I'll ask for a new pledge of allegiance.

"Send me Willbewill. I'll handle him. He may be dangerous. I'll have to butter him up a bit. He's the only one who—oh, it's you, Apollyon. About time you came."

"I heard about the emergency, sire. Came as soon as I could. The others are on their way."

"We must keep the news from getting in, Apollyon."

"What if it does? Some of it is bound to trickle in."

"Twist it. Only thing to do. Twist it. Tell them Emmanuel is coming to destroy instead of to save. Tell them they'll lose their liberty. You have to know how to handle these things with finesse. Will is the only one—"

"You are the master of the spurious, sire."

"Yes. That's why I'm king of Mansoul. Will is the only one who can turn the tide."

"Who, sire?"

"Willbewill." Diabolus turned to an underling. "Let me know when Willbewill arrives."

"Lord Willbewill *has* arrived, sire. He is waiting in your anteroom now."

"Good. Show him in. And get me a ghostwriter to write me a speech. I'm going to address the people of Mansoul in the market square."

Apollyon started for a side door.

"All of you stand by. Tell the others," said Diabolus after him, "we have one thing in our favor."

"And that is?"

"That Mansoul still has free will." They stared at each other for a long moment.

"Close the door after you," said Diabolus finally.

HEN WILLBEWILL ENTERED, DIABOLUS WAS SITTING BEHIND HIS DESK, RUBBING HIS HANDS TOGETHER. HIS EYES HAD PALED, HIS FACE WAS CONFIDENT AND SERENE, HIS VOICE OILY.

"Sit down, M'Lord," he said pleasantly, and pushed the box of cigars forward. "Best imported brimstone. I have them made in my own country."

"There's a bit of a hubbub—thank you. A bit of a hubbub about, sire," said Willbewill settling himself. "Don't know when I've ever seen it so busy in the castle."

"Willbewill, I sent for you over a matter of grave concern. I need your help," said Diabolus, getting right to business and leaning forward in a gesture that took Willbewill into his confidence and made them co-conspirators; it was most flattering. Willbewill leaned forward too, unaware that he was doing so.

"I hear rumors," Diabolus went on, "that Mansoul is about to be reduced to bondage again."

"No."

"Yes. I think, M'Lord, it can be no welcome news to you; I'm sure it's none to me."

"Shaddai?"

"Shaddai and his son, Emmanuel," Diabolus explained. "I do hope they are but flying stories," he added, "but we cannot be too careful. I think we'd be wise to nip all such rumors that tend to trouble our people."

"I agree."

"Good. Then here's what I want you to do. First, guards at every gate. As keeper of the gates, that's your responsibility. Anyone coming to Mansoul to trade, any propaganda coming in by any means, must be examined carefully and allowed in only if it is favorable to my—our excellent government."

"Yes, sire."

"And spies roving the streets within; let them have power to suppress and destroy anyone plotting against us or prattling about Shaddai and Emmanuel."

"Yes, master."

"The mind grows by what it feeds on."

"Well spoken, master."

"We're having a rally in the market square, I'm addressing the townfolk. Be there, Will. I need you."

Willbewill felt himself dismissed. He bolted for the door, elated with this new conspiratorial intimacy with his master. At the door he turned.

"It will be a great speech, sire," he blurted out, and departed to carry out his orders.

"It'll be the finest piece of double-talk that can be manufactured on such short notice," muttered Diabolus as he pulled a bell cord and reached for his scratch pad.

The market square was teeming with townspeople; everyone had turned out. The speech was indeed impressive.

Diabolus reminded them that they were his faithful subjects and reiterated their many liberties and privileges and joys under his rule, amid great cheering and hullabaloo. Then there was a stunned silence as he told them solemnly that King Shaddai was raising an army to come and destroy them. His voice dropped to a dramatic low as he mused that he, of course, could shift for himself and escape, and then rose to an impassioned cry as he protested that nay, he would never leave them. While they were trembling on the brink of tears with the wonderfulness of it all he pled for a new oath of loyalty and with a sob in his voice begged them to stand or fall with him. Then they cried out as one man, "Whoever will not stand with Diabolus, let him die the death!"

"Then let me remind you," Diabolus answered, "I do not promise you an easy time. It is vain for us to hope for quarter, Shaddai will not give it. And no matter what he says, do not believe it. You'll never live with him in pleasure as you live with me. You will be bound by laws that will pinch you and be made to do things that are hateful to you. But with us—"

There was a great roar from the crowd.

"I'm for you and you're for me!" he cried. The roar swelled to even greater proportions. This was the psychological moment.

"And so," he finished, "to your arms! Up and to your arms! In my castle is armor that will make you invincible to the onslaught of the enemy. There are helmets, breastplates, swords and shields and what-not to make you fight like men. I have samples here."

They quieted to a pin-drop silence and all strained to see.

"Allow me. My helmet." He held it high for all to see.

"This helmet is hope-of-getting-by-as-you-are-and-doing-well-at-last, no matter what kind of lives you live. It's a piece of approved armor, and it has never failed to work. As long as you keep this on, no sword, arrow or dart of Emmanuel can get you. And now—

"My breastplate. This is a breastplate of iron. I had it forged in my own country. We swear by it. In plain language, it's a hard heart—as hard as iron and as without feeling as a stone. Keep it on and mercy won't win you or judgment won't scare you. Most necessary. Yessss. And allow me—

"My sword. It's an evil tongue, to speak evil of Shaddai, his son, his ways and his people. Oh, it's devastating. Wonderful for offensive warfare. Then of course—

"My shield. It's unbelief. Use it to question the truth of Shaddai's word. Question everything Shaddai says. Don't think about it, *question* it. The worst thing you can do is take time to think. Those who have written of the wars of Emmanuel against my servants have testified that he could do no mighty work there because of their shield of unbelief. It has done much to promote my cause. And last—"

He paused dramatically for effect. "A-dumb-and-prayerless-spirit. Yes, in order to use my armor properly, your *attitude* must be right. It's as much a part of my armor as these other pieces. Everything's in the attitude. You must scorn to cry for mercy. What! Cry for mercy? Bah. Where's your pride? Where's your self-respect? Where's the dignity of man and the spark of divinity in your soul? Mercy? Never!"

This really got to them; they were quite carried away. He had to signal for them to quiet down so he could finish.

"Besides all this I have firebrands, arrows and death, all

good hand weapons. You'll be taught to use them.

"In closing, remember that I am your rightful king; you are under oath to me. Remember also the privileges, profits and honors I have endowed you with. Now is the time for you to show me your appreciation and loyalty. Stand fast, overcome this one shock, and I have no doubt but in time all the world will be ours. When that day comes I will make you kings, princes and captains. What brave days we shall have then!"

The cheering was close to hysteria, and when it died down: "That is all," Diabolus said. "An intensive program of training will go into effect at once. I declare Mansoul in a state of emergency!"

The crowd broke up, every man feeling already like a soldier. The streets were filled with officers of Diabolus' army.

"How did I do?" said Diabolus, on the way back to the castle.

"It was monstrous," said Beelzebub. "You were never better."

"They did not stick or boggle. As if it had been a sprat in the mouth of a whale, they swallowed it without any chewing," said Apollyon.

"I especially liked the 'you'll be bound by laws that pinch' part," said Legion. "I think that carried a lot of weight."

"It always does, it always does," Diabolus said with satisfaction. "But it's when I get to expounding on the dignity of man and the spark of divinity in the soul that I know I have it made. They love that."

"You forgot one thing," said Beelzebub.

"I did?"

"Yes. You forgot to shout 'Gardyloo!'* before you began."


Diabolus lost no time in putting Mansoul into intensive training for warfare. Every citizen was called into service in some capacity. They were thoroughly trained to use all the accouterments of warfare—the helmet of the hope-of-getting-by-as-you-are-and-doing-well-at-last, the breastplate of the hard heart, and the sword of the evil tongue, the shield of unbelief. And as they practiced and drilled, the-attitude-of-a-dumb-and-prayerless-spirit became a way of life.

Willbewill came and went, bustling and important, a dapper figurehead, respected by all in town. Mr. Conscience was up-again, down-again—his naps were longer; he was no bother to anyone. Lord Understanding bumbled about in his castle in darkness. Everyone went his own way and did what seemed right in his own sight.

Now all of this was accomplished none too soon, for already the first part of King Shaddai's great army was on the way.

---

* Cry used in old England to warn passers-by to avoid slops thrown from a window.

ORERUNNERS! HARBINGERS OF TID-
INGS! FOUR OF SHADDAI'S DIVISIONS
SENT AHEAD TO BREAK THE ICE AND
PAVE THE WAY—FORTY THOUSAND
STRONG!

The first division was under the great Captain Boanerges,
so called because he was a powerful orator. His standard-
bearer was Mr. Thunder who carried a black banner and had
three burning thunderbolts on his shield.

Then came Captain Conviction, that great prover of guilt;
indeed no guilt could stand up under his stern look. Mr.
Sorrow was his standard-bearer and he carried pale colors.
On the shield was an open book of the Law.

Next, Captain Judgment. His middle name was Punishment; his standard-bearer, Mr. Terror, who carried a red
banner and a picture of a fiery furnace on his shield.

Captain Execution brought up the rear. With Mr. Justice
carrying the banner, and wearing a shield showing Shaddai's
justice carried out—a tree with no fruit, and an ax lying at the
roots.

Forty thousand strong they were, with orders to offer
Mansoul peace terms at first. But each captain knew that if

they would not listen to peace terms and turn to King Shaddai, Mansoul would have to be taken by force.

On, on they marched, colors flying, helmets gleaming in the sun, a beautiful and awful sight to behold—ten thousand, twenty thousand, thirty thousand, forty thousand strong—on business for *the king!*

The people of Mansoul saw them coming in the distance, their glittering armor sparkling like jewels. The Mansoulians came out of their houses, and called out to each other, and stood on the city walls to see better. So gallant a company! So bravely accoutered! So excellently disciplined! The word spread and the crowds on the wall grew.

Diabolus saw them, too, from his castle. He stared for a while through his field glasses, his face contorted in a horrible grimace. Then, without a word, he handed the glasses to Apollyon who was standing near. "Hmmmm. Four divisions," Apollyon said. "They look as though they mean business."

"Yes." Diabolus motioned impatiently for the field glasses, took them, looked again. "They look good. There's Judgment. And Execution. Conviction's there, too. Good thing old man Conscience is in a coma."

"Who's the other one? There are four."

"Boanerges. He's the chap we'll have the most trouble with right now. Terrific orator. Voice like thunder. Scare hell out of anybody."

"What do you think they're going to do?"

"Well, they didn't come all this way for nothing. I think they'll pitch their tents and entrench themselves one way or another in a position of strength, and probably assault Eargate."

"They look good," Apollyon said again.

"They look too good," said Diabolus. "Those fool townfolk might forget everything I ever taught them, and let them in, on impulse."

"What should we do?"

"The main thing is to keep them from hearing Boanerges." Diabolus stared a moment longer, then whirled around, started for his bell cord. "The immediate thing to do is to get them down from the city walls. They shouldn't stand there staring. That display is pretty impressive." He pulled the cord. "I'll get them back down and into the market square."

"Are you going to mobilize them?"

"No, just talk to them, for the present. Then we'll see."


Down in the market square Diabolus addressed them with just the right amount of feigned concern, patience, amused tolerance and a wee bit of sternness. It was most effective. His voice had not been so oily since he had first descended upon them in the form of a dragon.

"Gentlemen—my beloved friends," he began. "I cannot but chide you a little for your uncircumspect action in going out to gaze on that great and mighty force entrenched outside the town. That display of banners and glittering armor you've been admiring is not there for your amusement. Do you know who they are? Where they come from? What they're up to?"

They were silent, waiting.

You *should* know. I told you, long ago. They are part of the very army that Shaddai has sent to destroy you." He paused for effect, just long enough. Then his voice rang out,

"When you first saw them, why didn't you fire the beacons and alarm the town?"

They shifted uneasily, stole glances at the city wall, and back at him.

"Why do you suppose I have commanded a watch, doubled the guards? Why have I armed you from head to foot? Why have I put you through training to make you as hard as iron with hearts like millstones? So you might go out like a company of innocents to gaze at them?"

They stood still, mesmerized.

"No!" he shrieked. "To *resist* them!"

This had such an effect that it was almost as though they took a step backward as one man. Diabolus knew just when to shift moods. He played them like an organ. His voice went back down to pianissimo. "I will rebuke you no further; I will chide you gently, however; let me never see such actions again. Let not one of you so much as show his head over the wall of the town of Mansoul without an order obtained from me. You have heard me. Now do as I tell you. And if you do, I can dwell here securely with you. And I can take care of not only myself, but *your* safety and honor also."

They were all silent for a moment. Then, "That is all," he said quietly, and turned with his war lords and officials and started back to the castle. It was far more effective than an impassioned ending might have been.

"You left them stunned and gaping," said Beelzebub later, back in the castle.

"They're not stunned and gaping now," said Apollyon. He was standing by one of the great windows, gazing down into the streets. "They seem to have panicked."

"Exactly," said Diabolus calmly. "When they listen to

me, they turn against Shaddai. They can't trust us both at once. It wouldn't make sense.''

Sounds drifted up from the crowds milling about in the streets.

"What are they saying?" said Diabolus.

"Something about the men that turned the world upside down have come here also," said Apollyon.

"And destroyers of our peace, or words to that effect," said Legion.

"This I like," said Diabolus. "This I like very well. This is just as I would have it. If we can just hold them there, let Shaddai's—''

He stopped.

The round clear notes of a trumpet came over the wall from the direction of Ear-gate. They listened, silent, until it had died away.

"Summons for a hearing," said Legion.

"That's Boanerges' trumpeter. Name's Take-Heed-What-You-Hear," said Diabolus. They waited.

"Anybody on the wall?" said Diabolus after a while.

"No," said Apollyon. "Nobody's going to answer."

"As I was saying," said Diabolus, "if we can just hold them there, then let Shaddai's captains take the town if they can."

"But isn't a confrontation eventually inevitable?" said Legion.

"Probably," said Diabolus, "but I still have a few tricks up my sleeve." He pulled a bell cord.

"What now?" they wanted to know.

"Remember old Unbelief?"

"Who?"

"Unbelief. One of my aldermen. Stout fellow."

"What does he have to do with this?"

"He," said Diabolus, "is one of the tricks. I've had my eye on him for some time. I'm going to appoint him mayor to replace Lord Lustings, temporarily."

*"Mayor?"*

"Yes. He has always impressed me as a good man to use in an emergency."

"Well?"

"Well I think we're about due for one," said Diabolus. And he pulled the bell cord again.

# WAR

IABOLUS WAS RIGHT; THE EMERGENCY WAS NOT FAR OFF.

CAPTAIN BOANERGES' TRUMPETER RE-TURNED AND REPORTED THAT MANSOUL would not answer the summons. The captain was grieved, but bade the trumpeter go to his tent.

A short time later the summons to a hearing was repeated. Again Mansoul would not answer. Then the captains and other field officers called a council of war, to consider what might be done. They decided to try one more summons.

This third summons was louder than the others; it seemed to demand an answer.

Sure enough Willbewill's head appeared over the wall.

"Who are you?" he cried. "Why are you making such a hideous noise? And what do you want?"

"I come in the name of Captain Boanerges and your former king, the great King Shaddai, whom you have rebel-led against. My master the captain has a special message for this town. Will you hear it peaceably?"

"I'll deliver your message to my master, Diabolus, and see what he has to say."

52

"The message is not for Diabolus; it's for Mansoul, in the name of the King."

"I'll deliver your message—eh, to the town, then."

"Captain Boanerges himself will be here to receive your answer," the trumpeter cried. And the interview was ended for the time being. Each went back to his master and reported what had happened.

When the time was up and the trumpet sounded again, not only Captain Boanerges, but the other captains and the entire four divisions were outside Ear-gate. Everybody who was anybody was on the city wall.

Captain Boanerges stepped forward. "I desire to speak with your mayor!" he shouted.

There was a slight hesitation, then a brief hubbub, then Unbelief stepped forward and boldly glared at the captain.

Boanerges started in surprise. "This is not the mayor," he shouted. "Where is Lord Mayor Understanding? I would deliver my message to him!"

Diabolus could keep quiet no longer. "My dear captain." His voice was dripping with mock patience. "You have summoned Mansoul to surrender to your king no less than four times. I don't know who gave you this authority and I don't intend to dispute that now. I merely ask what you are up to—or don't you know?"

Captain Boanerges paid him the crowning insult: He ignored him as if he were not there and addressed himself to the townsmen. He stood by the shield with the thunderbolts on, while his black banner rippled in the breeze behind him, and gave them the message again—to submit to King Shaddai.

Then Captain Conviction stepped forward. "Hear, O

Mansoul!'' he cried. ''It is your wisdom—it will be your happiness to surrender to Shaddai. You cannot claim you have not sinned; your very rebellion against him is your sin. All of your doings will testify against you.''

''Stop badgering them,'' cried Unbelief.

Conviction ignored him. ''Shaddai is reasoning with you through us,'' he cried to Mansoul. ''Does he have the need of you that you have of him? No, no! He is merciful and would not have you die, but turn to him and live. Do not overstay the time of mercy. Listen now!''

Then Captain Judgment stood forth. ''Do not underestimate the power of King Shaddai,'' he said. ''He is able to lay you at his feet. O Mansoul, he is holding out his golden scepter to you; will you provoke him to shut his gates against you instead? Don't refuse his mercy now; he is preparing his throne for judgment later.''

Diabolus trembled. Some saw; most did not notice.

Captain Execution stepped forward. ''Every tree that does not bear good fruit,'' he said, ''is hewn down and cast into the fire. The ax is first laid to your root by way of threatening. Ultimately it must be laid *at* your root by way of execution. Between these two is required your repentance. Shaddai's patience does not last forever. Your rebellion has brought this army to your walls; what makes you think Shaddai cannot carry out his words?''

There was silence.

Then some murmuring started in the crowd and grew louder until a few braver spokesmen called out, ''Time! The Mansoulians want a little time to consider their answer!'' The request was timid; it was obvious that the Mansoulians had no leaders among themselves.

"We'll give you time on one condition," shouted Boanerges. "That you throw Mr. Ill-Pause over the wall to us. If you hesitate a moment with him in town, you are lost. Now! Over the top!"

This threat galvanized Diabolus into action. Lose Ill-Pause? Never! He forgot his momentary fright. He leaped forward. "Give these villains an answer!" he ordered his officers. "Speak out! You, Unbelief—you first!"

Unbelief was ready. "You have camped against us, but where you came from we don't know and your promises of mercy and threats of judgment from this king you say sent you here, make a pretty tall story. We do not believe you. We're not afraid of you. We defy you and your summons. Now get you gone, bag and baggage, before our weapons start flying from the city walls against you!"

Diabolus turned to Willbewill. "Come, come," he hissed. "Willbewill! Speak out! Speak!"

Willbewill swallowed hard; he was desperate. "Ah— yes," he said. "That is right. All that he says. We have heard your demands and your threats. We're not afraid of you. We defy you and your summons. Besides we prefer to remain as we are. And we give you three days to get out!" For the first time the horrible suspicion that he might be a "yes-man" crossed his mind, but there wasn't time to dwell on it. Mr. Forget-Good, the new town recorder, was speaking without prompting.

"Gentlemen," he said, "we have answered your rough and angry demands with mild and gentle words: And we've given you leave to depart quietly as you came. Now take our kindness and be gone. We might have come out with force against you and given you a bit of trouble, but as we love quiet and ease ourselves, we do not wish to hurt or molest others.''

For some strange reason the townspeople took that as a signal to shout for joy, as though a great victory had already been won. They began to ring bells and make merry, and even danced upon the walls.

Diabolus and his war lords exchanged smug glances.

''They did a good job of it,'' said Beelzebub.

''Couldn't have done better myself,'' said Diabolus.

''You had very little to say,'' said Legion.

''I believe in democracy,'' said Diabolus, ''upon occasion. Sometimes it's better to let them speak for themselves.''

They started back to the castle. Lord Mayor Unbelief went back to his place. And Mr. Forget-Good the recorder, to his.

But Lord Willbewill stayed behind to do his homework. He took special care that the gates were secured with double guards, double bolts, and double locks and bars, especially Ear-gate. He shouted orders and huffed and puffed and paced about. And still not satisfied, he made old Mr. Prejudice, one of the ''angry old men'' of the town, captain of Ear-gate with sixty deaf men under him. This last thing done, he went back to the top of the tower over Ear-gate to check two of Mansoul's great guns; one was called High-mind and the other Heady. These had been cast in the castle by Diabolus' founder whose name was Mr. Puff-Up, and Mansoul set great store by them.

Then Willbewill made his way wearily back to his home. One could not be too zealous.

Behind him the merriment on the walls grew noisier. There was, strangely, something ominous about it. Willbewill shivered in the twilight. Then, through the shouts and the ringing of the bells and the noisemakers, he heard it: The battle cry of Shaddai's captains.

Lord Lustings heard it, and old Unbelief heard it, and Mr. Forget-Good too heard it, from their houses. And Diabolus and his war lords heard it from the castle.

The cry rang loud and clear through the twilight air and penetrated every barracks, every castle, every home.

"YE MUST BE BORN AGAIN!"

Willbewill turned up the collar of his cloak and hurried toward his home, repelled by the words. And a little frightened, though he would not admit it.

The war was on.

RUMPETS WERE BLOWN, AND THE KING'S ARMY LEAPED INTO ACTION. BANNERS WAVED, AND FROM FORTY THOUSAND MEN THE BATTLE CRY WENT UP, "YE MUST BE BORN AGAIN."

The war was on, indeed.

The actual fighting started out in low key, like the muted rumbling of distant thunder, then rose and swelled and subsided and rose and swelled again, taking enough surprise turns to boggle the imagination.

There were minor skirmishes at first, with both sides hoping to keep it down to this scale and prevent escalation if possible. It was in one of these skirmishes that Willbewill sallied forth, fell in upon the rear of Captain Boanerges' men and captured three prisoners. He delivered them eagerly to Diabolus, glad of a chance to reinstate himself, for he still felt rather a fool for the hesitant way he had conducted himself on the city wall.

"Who are you?" said Diabolus, when they were brought before him. The question was a matter of form; he already knew.

58

"Mr. Tradition, sire."

"Mr. Human-Wisdom, sire."

"Mr. Man's-Invention, sire."

"You don't sound like the king's men," said Diabolus. "Are you proselytes?"

"Well, hardly," said Mr. Tradition.

"We came upon Shaddai's captains while they were on their way here, and offered our services," said Mr. Human-Wisdom.

"Actually," said Mr. Man's-Invention, "we do not live so much by religion as by the fates of fortune. Which ever way the wind blows, you know."

"Ah yes," said Diabolus.

"And if you are willing to entertain us—"

"You are willing to serve me. Yes. I understand," said Diabolus. He was already scribbling a note. "I'm sending you to one of my captains. He will take care of you. You will be made at least sergeants. Perhaps even armor-bearers."

He handed Willbewill the note. "Will you escort them and see that they get quartered and settled?" he said. Willbewill took the note and departed in a bustle with his charges, with ruffling words and much heel clicking.

"Who'd you send them to?" said Beelzebub, after they had left.

"Captain Anything, naturally," said Diabolus.

"Naturally," said Beelzebub.



A week later the explosion occurred.

The king's men had managed to dismount the two guns on

59

the tower over Ear-gate—the guns called High-mind and Heady.

The townsmen answered with shout against shout, charge against charge. New officers were thrown into the front lines; Mr. Puff-Up; Sergeant Prejudice, Captain Anything (who had for his armor-bearer Mr. Man's-Invention), and, yes, Sergeant Tradition and Sergeant Human-Wisdom. With battering rams, with slings, with guns, with swords, the battle raged—but Ear-gate could not be broken down. The casualties began to mount.

One good shot blasted a hole in the roof of Lord Mayor Understanding's castle and let in some light. Lord Willbewill was almost killed outright with a sling, but he recovered. Many of the aldermen were slain. Other guns were dismounted and laid flat in the dirt. But Ear-gate held fast.

When the great battle was over and the smoke cleared, the awful truth was that the first round belonged to Mansoul. The king's captains retreated to their winter quarters, a safe distance away. It was all over but the shouting.

But nobody in the town felt like shouting. Something had happened to Mansoul. Even though the townspeople were safe inside they could not sleep. They tried to be merry again. "Look," they told themselves, "we can do anything we want to. There is no limit, no law, no censorship, there are no restrictions at all!"

But the things that they could do had somehow lost their appeal.

Alarm flares kept going up from the camp of Shaddai's army; they could be seen from Mansoul all too well. The nights were the worst. Sometimes Captain Conviction would take all ten thousand of his men and run around the walls of the town all night, shouting the battle cry—"YE MUST BE BORN AGAIN!"

These alarms from without had a wearing-down effect on the townfolk of Mansoul. And out of their weariness came whispers—"We cannot go on like this"—and—"Perhaps we *should* return to King Shaddai and end our troubles"—and, in fear—"But would he take us now?"

But by some strange coincidence, these alarms had a stimulating effect on old Mr. Conscience. He would not, could not be drugged anymore, but began to roar with a voice of thunder that shook the whole town and set everyone atrembling. There was no noise now so terrible to Mansoul as the voice of Conscience and the shoutings of the captains.

Certain things began to grow scarce in Mansoul, reaching the proportions of famine. Upon all her pleasant things there was a blast, and burning instead of beauty. Wrinkles now, and some shows of the shadow of death were on the inhabitants. They would have gladly exchanged anything they had for peace of mind.

Peace of mind! Shaddai's captains kept sending summons by Take-Heed-What-You-Hear, Boanerges' trumpeter, to add to Mansoul's misery. The first time he treated them gently, then a little more roughly. The third time he dealt with them very roughly, telling them he did not know whether the captains were inclining to mercy or judgment. It was this third summons that precipitated the parley.

"A parley!"

The cry rang out and the good news spread quickly all over town. Yes, they were going to talk peace! The officials of Mansoul were even now drawing up the terms under which they would surrender.

The day was set. The crowds gathered and waited eagerly as the trumpet sounded. The captains came up in their harness, with their ten thousands at their feet. And it was announced that the townsmen had heard and considered the summons and would come to an agreement with them and with their King Shaddai upon certain terms that Diabolus had ordered them to propound. Then the conditions were read by Willbewill.

"These be our conditions of peace," he bellowed. "We will submit to King Shaddai upon the following conditions:

"One. That our own officials still rule and govern Mansoul.

"Two. That no man now serving under Diabolus be cast out.

"Three. That we may still enjoy certain rights and privileges granted us under our master, Diabolus.

"Four. That no new law or officer have power over us without our consent!"

Captain Boanerges, who had stiffened at the first condition, stepped forward. His voice was low but it carried to the farthest listener. "Oh, inhabitants of Mansoul—when I first heard your trumpet sound for a parley with us, I was glad. When you said you were willing to submit yourselves to our king and lord, I was yet more joyous; but when, by your silly provisos and foolish quibbling, you laid the stumblingblock of your iniquity before your own faces, my joy was turned to fear for you!" His voice rose. "I perceive that old Ill-Pause had a hand in drawing up those proposals! They are not fit to be heard by anyone who even pretends to serve Shaddai! In the name of my king I refuse and reject your conditions with the highest disdain!"

Mansoul was shocked into silence.

"But, O Mansoul—" Boanerges' voice turned to pleading—"if you will but give yourselves into the hands of our king and trust him to make the terms, his terms will be profitable to you; trust yourself to Shaddai. He demands nothing less than unconditional surrender!"

"Unconditional surrender?" Old Unbelief leaped forward. "Consider what you're doing. Who would be so foolish as to take the staff out of his own hands and put it into the hands of someone who wants such complete submission?" He turned frantically to the Mansoulians. "If you once yield, if you give yourselves up to another, you are no longer your own. To give yourselves up to an unlimited power is the greatest folly! folly! folly!" His voice seemed to ricochet along the walls and echo and reecho endlessly and the Mansoulians stood there stunned and silent, listening.

That did it.

After the silence, they all began to talk at once; they were thrown into confusion; beyond all hope of reaching an agreement.

When the officials returned to the castle, Diabolus was waiting and he was delighted. He slapped old Unbelief on the back as they went into the Chamber of State. "M'Lord Mayor," he said, "my faithful Unbelief. What a remarkable job you did! If we ever get through this mess I shall one day make you my—my Universal Deputy. Yes. Why not? How would you like that? I hear you even kept Understanding and that old fool Conscience from being at the parley. Oh, you clever, clever—Here. Have a cigar. Imported brimstone. Take the whole box. My Universal Deputy some day, yes. Next to me, you'll have all nations under your hand. Nor shall any of our vassals walk more at liberty than those that shall be content to walk in your fetters.''

Mayor Unbelief left the Chamber of State, his head in the clouds with dreams of future power. Imagine! Universal Deputy! So puffed up was he that he did not see the mob coming toward him until they were almost upon him.

He opened his mouth to speak, then stopped, stunned. They were headed by Lord Understanding! And Mr. Conscience! Impossible! But it was so! And they were angry!

He stopped, drew himself up to his full height and prepared to quash their wrath with the bigness and the show of his countenance. But they would not be quashed; they came on, running. He decided to run too. He turned and fled, they upon his heels, until he came to his house, where he slipped in through the front door, bolted it behind him, and decided that he could address them with more dignity from an upper window. In a moment he popped his head out. ''Where'd *you* come from? Who let *you* out?'' he bawled. And then he got hold of himself.

''Gentlemen, *gentlemen*,'' he asked, ''what is the reason for this uproar?''

Lord Understanding stepped forward. ''You would not let Mr. Conscience and me be at the parley!'' he cried. ''You propounded terms of peace that could not possibly be accepted without making King Shaddai a mere figurehead. And you charged Shaddai's captains with treachery when they offered mercy!''

''Treason, treason!'' Unbelief shouted. ''To your arms, oh trusty friends of Diabolus!''

''Call it treason if you like,'' said Understanding. ''But those captains deserved better treatment at your hands.''

"I spoke for my prince!" wailed Unbelief.

"Stop the dramatics," old Mr. Conscience broke in, "and don't answer the mayor like that. He has spoken the truth. And don't be so impudent; you have caused enough grief. If you'd accepted the conditions, we would not be in a state of war right now!"

"Watch it," cried Unbelief. "I'll report you to Diabolus, and you'll have an answer to your words. Meanwhile we'll seek the good of the town without any help from you."

"You and Diabolus are imposters!" cried Understanding. "*You* seek the good of the town?"

"Treason!" shouted Unbelief again, and he leaned so far out he nearly fell from his window.

His cries brought results. Lord Willbewill and Mr. Prejudice and several aldermen and burgesses, and even old Ill-Pause himself, came running up to ask the reason of the hubbub. With that, everybody began to talk at once and no one could be heard distinctly.

"Hold it! *Hold* it!" Unbelief bellowed.

There was a sudden silence.

"M'Lord," said Unbelief to Willbewill. Now his voice could have been spread on a cracker, "There are a couple of peevish gentlemen here who have, as the fruit of their bad dispositions, I fear, gathered a mob against me and caused this tumult. It is not myself alone that I care for, but methinks they are attempting to run the town into acts of rebellion against our prince."

"It's preposterous!"

"Mutiny!"

"Call it mutiny, then. We'll fight!"

And they did. *First words—*

"Take them to prison!"

"Oh no you won't!"

"Unbelief, live forever!"

"The devil he will; we'll chop him down now!"

"Down with censorship! Up with Mr. Forget-Good!"

"Long live Mr. Conscience!"

"Shaddai's captains would ruin our economy!"

"Shaddai's captains offered us mercy!"

*Then blows—*

Wooosh! Old Conscience was knocked down twice by Mr. Benumbing. But for a poor aim, Lord Understanding would have been slain with a musket. But it wasn't all one-sided.

Wop! Mr. Mind beat the brains out of Mr. Rash-Head. Old Mr. Prejudice was kicked, thrown in the dirt, and had his crown cracked to boot. Captain Anything wasn't popular on either side because he'd never been true to anyone. He was pushed back and forth from one side to the other. He got one of his legs broken, and some wished it had been his neck.

Oh—what a fight! What a futile, useless fight.

Lord Willbewill was seen to smile when he saw old Prejudice tumble in the dirt. When Captain Anything came halting up to him, he seemed to take but little notice. He really did not take one side more than the other.

But Willbewill was no match for Diabolus, nor was Mansoul. Fighting within, confusion was the old master's best weapon, and turning Mansoul's best efforts into shambles his genius. With all this awakening, it was a shameful page in their history that Mansoulians listened to him again. But after the dust settled, they did.

Diabolus finally threw Conscience and Lord Understanding in prison, made another speech full of double-talk on liberty, and reduced them all to simpering idiots again.

Ear-gate remained closed.

Blind, blind Mansoul. It could not stand up against Diabolus or resist his wiles. And so its bravest efforts went down in defeat.

But far far away, over the hills and plains, another army was marching—marching to aid the four brave captains outside the city walls. An army headed by none other than Prince Emmanuel himself. An army that could not be resisted.

No—Mansoul was no match for Diabolus—but Emmanuel was!

N ARMY THAT COULDN'T BE RESISTED, MARCHING TOWARD THE TOWN OF MANSOUL! AN ARMY HEADED BY NONE OTHER THAN KING SHADDAI'S SON, PRINCE EMMANUEL!

In their quarters, Shaddai's captains heard the tidings from the forerunners, sent ahead to bring the good news. They delivered up a shout of joy that rent the earth and made the mountains shake. And they made preparations to send a party out to meet him.

In the town of Mansoul, things went on as usual. They felt the trembling of the earth and heard the shouts, but they were so completely engrossed in their own pleasures and lusts that they scarcely paid them any heed.

In the Chamber of State, Diabolus sat hunched over his desk, surrounded by his war lords.

"Do they know in the town?" said Beelzebub.

"They are not concerned," said Diabolus. "They are woefully besotted now and completely indifferent, thanks to our strategy."

"And you?" said Apollyon.

"I have felt the weight of Emmanuel's hand already," said Diabolus glumly. "I know better than to be indifferent." He rose heavily and went over to one of the large windows, wiped away some cobwebs and strained his eyes to see across the plains. Legion brought over some field glasses and they all followed and huddled there by the windows, watching.

What an army!

First, the noble Captain Faith. His were the red colors and his standard-bearer was Mr. Promise. On his shield was the holy Lamb with the golden shield.

Next came the famous Captain Good-Hope. His were the blue colors and his standard-bearer was Mr. Expectation. On his shield he had the three golden anchors.

The third was the valiant captain, Captain Love. His were the green colors and his standard-bearer was Mr. Merciful. On his shield he had three naked orphans.

The fourth was that gallant commander, Captain Guile-less. His standard-bearer was Mr. Harmless and his were the white colors. On his shield he had three golden doves.

The fifth and last was Captain Patience. His standard-bearer was Mr. Suffer-Long and his were the black colors. On his shield he had three arrows through the golden heart.

Each captain had ten thousand men under him. And the prince headed them all, riding in his chariot.

Oh, how their trumpets sounded and how their armor glittered and how their colors waved in the wind! The prince's armor was all of gold and it shone like the sun. The captains' armor was of silver and were like the glittering stars. And they came prepared to fight; they had battering rams and slings, all made of pure gold—sixty-six in all.

When they got to the camp, another shout went up, louder than before.

"What will you do?" asked Diabolus' war lords.

"Watch—and, for now, wait," said Diabolus. "I'll

think of something when the time comes." But the very castle was trembling under their feet.

Emmanuel's army began to beset the town. They surrounded it. They cast up mounts against it, and small banks. Mount Gracious. Mount Justice. Plain-truth Hill. No-sin Banks. And the slings and battering rams were placed on these mounts and banks—the biggest on Mount Hearken, near Ear-gate. Whichever way Mansoul looked, it saw force and power lying in siege against it.

Then the preliminary operations began. Diabolus and his war lords watched from the castle. "There is a flag up on Mount Gracious," said Beelzebub, "offering mercy."

"So I see," said Diabolus.

"What do you think they'll do?"

"I don't expect them to do anything. The Mansoulians have the proper attitude. A dumb and prayerless spirit. 'Scorn to cry for mercy.' "

"And there goes a red flag on Mount Justice warning of judgment," said Apollyon.

"And a black flag threatening the execution of judgment," said Legion.

"They have my helmet; the 'hope-of-getting-by-as-you-are-and-doing-well-at-last,' " said Diabolus. "We're safe—if they've been doing their homework."

"There's no response."

"They've been doing their homework."

They kept close watch; Mansoul did not respond.

Then Emmanuel sent a messenger to explain to the Mansoulians what he meant by those signs and ceremonies of the flags, and to ask of them which of the things they would choose—grace and mercy, or judgment and the execution of judgment.

Some sort of an answer was clearly mandatory; one did not ignore Prince Emmanuel. But they were at their wits end as to what to answer. In a spurt of bravura they sent him a message saying that they did not make either peace or war without Diabolus and that they would petition him to go down to the wall and "there give you such treatment as he shall think fit and profitable for us." They were too far gone to realize what a pathetic picture they made, or how monstrous their airs were.

They they went to Diabolus. He huffed and puffed and tried to put them off by circumlocution. "But somebody has to answer him," they wailed, "and we don't know how." So in the end, he agreed to go down and answer. But he was afraid.

"I'll go down to the gates and give him such an answer as I think fit," he said. And he went down to Mouth-gate and addressed himself to Emmanuel, but in his own language so the town would not witness his humiliation.

"O great Emmanuel, lord of all," he said, "I know you, that you are the son of the great Shaddai. But why have you come here to torment me and to cast me out of my possession? This town of Mansoul, as you very well know, is mine. Mine by right of conquest; I won it. Mine by their say-so. They opened their gates to me. They've sworn fidelity to me and have openly chosen me to be their king. They have also given their castle over to me. Yes, they've *chosen* me." He crouched and cringed as he stood before Emmanuel, but he went on—"Moreover they have disavowed you. Yes, they've cast your law, your name, your seal and all that is yours behind their backs. Ask your captains! Ask them! They'll tell you what Mansoul's answers to all the summons have been. Loyalty to me and scorn to you!" His voice became whining now—"Now you are the just and holy one and should do no wrong. In the name of all that's just and holy, go away and leave me in peace!"

Emmanuel had waited through this twaddle. When it was quite finished, the golden prince stood up. "Mansoul yours by conquest?" he said. "Oh no. Yours by fraud, by lies, by deceit. You perverted the intent and purpose of my father's law. You overcame Mansoul by promising them happiness in their transgressions against my father's law, since you knew from your own experience that that was the way to undo them. Then you defaced my father's seal in Mansoul and set up your own. And then you stirred them up against my father's captains and made them fight against those who were sent to deliver them from their bondage."

Diabolus looked nervously back toward the town.

"I am not finished," said Emmanuel. Diabolus braced himself to stay.

"Mansoul is mine," Emmanuel went on. "Mine by inheritance from my father. My father built Mansoul with his own hands. The palace that is in the midst of that town he built for his own delight. And I am my father's heir and the only delight of his heart. His it was and he gave it to me. Mansoul is my desire, and the joy of my heart."

Diabolus was getting visibly uncomfortable.

"And Mansoul is mine by right of purchase," said Emmanuel. "I have bought it. Mansoul trespassed against my father, and my father had said that in the day that they broke his law, they would die. Now it is more possible for heaven and earth to pass away than for my father to break his word. Wherefore, when Mansoul listened to you and broke that law, I became a security to my father, for I would pay for Mansoul's sin, and my father accepted this security. So when the time appointed was come, I bore Mansoul's sin in my own body on the cross. And with Mansoul's sin upon me, my own father had to turn his back on me so that I cried out, 'My father, my father, why hast thou forsaken me?' And with Mansoul's sin upon me, I laid down my life. On the third day my father raised me from the dead; the transaction was completed.

"Nor did I do this by halves; my father's law and justice are both now satisfied and very well content that Mansoul should be delivered.

"But I have no more to say to you. I have a word for Mansoul."

"Not if I can help it," muttered Diabolus, and he slithered through the gate, back into town and began to issue frantic orders.

"O Mansoul, I am touched with compassion for you," Emmanuel called out, "you have opened your gates to Diabolus but have shut them fast against me. You have listened to him but have stopped your ears to my cry. He brought you destruction and you received both him and it; I have come to bring you salvation but you do not regard me. Listen to me, Mansoul, listen to my word and you will live. I am merciful, Mansoul. Do not shut me out of your gates. All my words are true; I am mighty to save!"

But the gates were locked and bolted and nobody heard him.

# NEGOTIATIONS

IAR!"

DIABOLUS' VOICE RANG THROUGH THE CASTLE AS HE BURST INTO THE FOYER. "LIAR!"

He made his way to the Chamber of State.

"Liar," he gasped, leaning against the door.

"Are you calling somebody one?" asked his war lords.

"No, I want one," he said. "Get me the biggest liar you can find."

"But, sire," they said, "you have that honor. You are the biggest liar in the Universe."

"Oh yes," he remembered. "I lost my head."

"Another council of war is advisable?" they wanted to know.

"Another council of war is inevitable," he said.

"Do you think Emmanuel's next move will be to fight?" said Beelzebub.

"I think he will get his battering rams and slings ready to assault Ear-gate and Eye-gate; certainly he will give us battle," said Diabolus. "But there is no way lawfully to take Mansoul except to get in by the gates."

"Well?"

"Well, I think he will give Mansoul another chance to surrender peaceably."

"What are you getting at, Sire?"

Diabolus walked over to the window, pushed the cobwebs aside and looked out, lost in thought.

"Perhaps it isn't a liar we want," he said at last. "Perhaps it's a good bargainer. Someone who can dicker. Yes. Someone who can dicker."

He turned around to face them. "The way I see it— Emmanuel gives Mansoul another chance to surrender peaceably. We call a council of war with the gentry of Mansoul. We draw up the propositions under which we'll surrender. Then I suggest that we send a representative—and I shall recommend one—out to Emmanuel's camp to submit the propositions. The propositions will of course be impossible for Emmanuel to accept. And we shall all be nicely at loggerheads again.

"You see," he finished, and he was his old self again, composed, cunning, confident, "we still have one great thing in our favor."

"And that is?"

"Free will. Shaddai has given Mansoul free will."

They thought about this for a moment.

"How about old Mr. Loath-To-Stoop?" said Apollyon.

"Excellent!" said Diabolus. "Stout fellow. Just the man for the job. Good thinking!" And he pulled a bell cord.


Mr. Loath-To-Stoop was an old man, a stiff man in his way, and a great doer for Diabolus. He went to the camp of

Emmanuel and a time was appointed to give him audience. When the time came, and after a Diabolonian ceremony or two, he got right to the point.

"Great Sire," he said, "that it might be known unto all men how good-natured a prince my master is, he has sent me to tell Your Lordship that he is willing, rather than escalate the war, to deliver up into your hands, one half of the town of Mansoul."

"The whole town is mine by gift and purchase," said Emmanuel, "I will not lose one half."

"Well, then, my master will be content that you shall have the title of Lord of All of Mansoul without being responsible for the duties associated with the job. And he'll possess just a part."

"Mansoul is mine in *reality*, not in name only. I will possess it all or none at all."

"Sire, behold the condescension of my master! He says that he'll be content if you'll assign to him some place in Mansoul to live privately in—any place you say. You'll be lord of the rest."

"All that my father gives me shall come to me; I will lose nothing. No, I'll not grant him the least corner."

"All right. You win. All the town is yours—with this proviso; that some times when he comes by this way, he may, for old acquaintance sake, be entertained as a wayfaring man for—oh, say two days—ten days—or a month or so. May not this small matter be granted?"

"No. He came as a wayfaring man to David, nor did he stay long with him; and yet it nearly cost David his soul. I will not consent even to that."

Mr. Loath-To-Stoop sighed. "You are very hard, Sire.

Suppose my master yields to all you've said—provided that his friends and relatives might have liberty just to trade in the town and enjoy their present homes. Now you *can't* refuse that.''

"I do refuse that. It is contrary to my father's will. Every Diabolonian must lose his land, his liberty, his life.''

"Ah me. May not my master maintain *some* kind of old friendship just with letters? Accidental opportunities and the like?''

"No, by no means. *Any* fellowship, even remote, will corrupt Mansoul and alienate its affections from me, and endanger its peace with my father.''

"Postcards?''

"No.''

"Just an occasional token of his love? To some of his old friends? So they might look back and remember merry times?''

"If Mansoul come to be mine, I shall not consent that there be one scrap or shred or even the dust of Diabolus left behind as tokens or gifts or remembrances.''

Mr. Loath-To-Stoop prepared for departure. "Well, Sire,'' he said with a briskness he did not feel, "I have one thing more to propose—then I'll go. Suppose that sometimes, someone in Mansoul has business—urgent business—that must be done in a certain way or the party will be—uh—undone, shall we say. And suppose, Sire, that nobody could help but my lord and master? He could be sent for, perhaps? Or the person could meet him outside and—uh—consult with him there?''

"They will have no business, no problems, that cannot be solved by my father. By prayer—by supplication—they will make their requests known to him. And to him alone. I will leave *no* door open, or even ajar, for Diabolus.''

"You are," sighed Mr. Loath-To-Stoop, "most inflexible. I shall take your answers to my lord.''

"There is only *one* answer.''

"Ah me. I shall take your—uh—answer then.''

And so Mr. Loath-To-Stoop departed, having stooped very, very low indeed, and without success.

He went straight to the castle. As the door to the Chamber of State was opened for him to be admitted, the draft sent the dust bunnies scurrying across the floor and the cobwebs that hung from the rafters and the window tops swaying to and fro. Diabolus and his war lords heard him to the end, without comment. Then there was a long glum silence.

"Send me Ill-Pause," said Diabolus finally. "Have him tell both the town and Prince Emmanuel that Mansoul and its king are resolved to stand or fall together; we won't give up without a fight.''

## SURRENDER AND SALVATION

IELD THE SWORD!
THE CRY RENT THE AIR; EMMANUEL
GAVE THE ORDERS. CAPTAIN
BOANERGES, CAPTAIN CONVICTION,
Captain Judgment and Captain Execution marched up to
Ear-gate with trumpets sounding, colors flying, and with
shouting for the battle. Captain Faith and Captain Good-Hope
and Captain Love joined them. The rest of Emmanuel's
captains and their men deployed themselves around the town
for the best advantages against the enemy. And the word was
given forth:

"EMMANUEL!"

Then an alarm was sounded in Mansoul and the battle
began. The slings whirled stones against the gates, against the
walls, over the walls and into the town. Every gate shuddered
under the fierce assault. The artillery roared and the dust rose
and the plains outside Mansoul trembled and the sky clouded
overhead and the market square within was jammed with
panic-stricken townfolk both fighting and getting in the way
of those fighting and the castle rocked on its foundations.

Wield the sword!

Captain Boasting was slain. Boasting, who thought that
nobody could have shaken the posts of Ear-gate.

Wield the sword!

Captain Secure was slain, and Captain Bragman, and Mr. Feeling, and Mr. Love-No-Good, though his death was lingering. And Willbewill was completely daunted, unable to do what he wanted to. His leg was badly wounded and his head was in a whirl.

Wield the sword!

Mr. Ill-Pause received a grievous wound in the head; some say that his brainpan was cracked. And old Mr. Prejudice fled, along with Captain Anything.

Diabolus made a desperate last-ditch stand.

"If it's peace and quiet you want, I have terms now you'll be pleased with!" he screamed to Emmanuel from the city wall.

"Nothing can be regarded that you propose," said Emmanuel. "Nothing is done by you but to deceive."

"Draw off your forces; I'll bend Mansoul to your bow!"

"How flexible and convenient are your ways," said Emmanuel. "How often you change and rechange."

"Make me your deputy; I'll persuade them to be religious. I'll show them where they have erred and that transgression stands in the way of life. I'll show them the holy law to which they must conform!"

"All the while knowing that man's greatest proficiency in keeping the law will amount to nothing," said Emmanuel.

"I'll make them reform!"

"You'll make them reform? *You* the head of that reformation? Diabolus a corrector of vice?"

"To make sure it all works, I myself, at my own expense, will set up and maintain a ministry! I promise you it will be sufficient!"

"Sufficient ministry?" said Emmanuel. "Who is sufficient? *My* grace is sufficient for my ministers. My strength is made perfect in their *weakness!*"

"Besides the ministry—"

"Now you would transform yourself into an angel of light and be a minister of righteousness," said Emmanuel. "And no wonder. You are too easy to recognize when you show your cloven hoof; but in white you are seen but by a few."

"Besides the ministry I'll set up lectures," Diabolus went on desperately. "Once a week!"

"I will set up my own standard."

*"Twice* a week!"

"I did not come to deliver Mansoul by works. I have come to reconcile them to my father."

Diabolus said nothing.

"Deceit was your first card, and it's the last card you have to play," said Emmanuel.

Diabolus just stared for a moment. "We understand each other," he said at last. "Deceit is the last card I have to play. There is nothing more to say."

"I will possess this town," continued Emmanuel, "and I will make it new and it shall be the glory of the Universe."

But Diabolus had turned away, his heart bursting with hate and rage.

Back in the town he screamed orders to his war lords.

"Muster your forces, muster your forces!"

"It's no use!" they cried, "we can't win!"

"Then fight the Mansoulians!" he shrieked. "Do what mischief you can in here!"

And the golden slings came faster and the artillery roared overhead and the battle cry got louder.

"MANSOUL IS WON!" Some of the townspeople were shouting.

At last Diabolus had to concede defeat. He rounded up his war lords and they made a dash for the castle. Just as they bolted the door they heard it.

"Ear-gate is broken open!"

The cry went through the town. "Ear-gate is broken open!" People scrambled up one street and down another, each heading for his own house. Their former champion, Diabolus, was nowhere to be found.

The town shook with the sound of trumpets and the shouts of victory—"Mansoul is won! Mansoul is won!" It also shook with battering rams and slings and stones, for the work was not all done yet.

From Ear-gate the street led straight through town and finally came to the house of Mr. Conscience. This was the way Prince Emmanuel chose to go, for Conscience's house was a vantage point from which to besiege the castle. The captains cleared that street by the use of their slings, and Captain Boanerges and Captain Conviction and Captain Judgment marched through the town with flying colors, to the town recorder's house. They did look warlike, for they took battering rams with them to plant against the gates. Everyone who saw them was terrified.

They marched right up to the gates, knocked and demanded entrance. Mr. Conscience was also terrified; at first he did not answer. Then—wop! went the battering ram and the whole house trembled and tottered. The old gentleman came down to the gates and with quivering lips he asked, "Who's there?" It was scarcely the voice of a warrior. Mansoul was plainly not in strong hands.

"We are the captains of great King Shaddai and Prince Emmanuel. We demand possession of your house for our noble prince." Boanerges punctuated this with another blow from the battering ram and Mr. Conscience, with trembling hands, opened the gates.

All that remained were the mopping-up operations. From the house of Mr. Conscience, it was an easy matter to besiege the castle. The great Diabolus was hauled out, shrinking and cringing, taken to the market square, and there, before all the townfolk, Emmanuel stripped him of his armor—the helmet (the hope-of-getting-by-as-you-are-and-doing-well-at-last), the breastplate (a hard heart), the shield of unbelief, the sword of an evil tongue, and the attitude-of-a-dumb-and-prayerless-spirit. As these weapons dropped to the ground and the townfolk saw them for what they really were, and as their prince Diabolus stood before them stripped of his glamorous accouterments and they saw him as he really was, they could only stare at the ground in dumb misery and shame.

Then Emmanuel got into his golden chariot, Diabolus was chained to the rear of it, and a great procession started slowly out of town. It included Emmanuel and all of his captains except two.

In silence the townfolk watched them all go. They clambered up on the city walls the better to see them, as the group crossed the plains outside. They watched as Diabolus was turned loose off in the distance. He walked away and they watched him until he was lost from view, over the horizon. The rumor spread through the crowd that he was turned loose to wander through the parched places in a salt land, seeking rest, but finding none.

They waited for Emmanuel to come back. There was a great silence; not one in the crowd dared speak. They just strained their eyes to see.

But Emmanuel did not come back.

They watched as he retired to the royal pavilion in his camp and in the midst of his father's forces. At first they could not believe it. They still waited, hoping he would emerge again in the distance. But he did not.

He was gone, and gone were all the glorious captains with him—the mighty Captain Faith, the famous Captain Good-Hope, the valiant Captain Love, the gallant Captain Guile-less, the noble Captain Patience, and two of Shaddai's captains too—who were they? Captain Judgment and Captain Execution. Who was left?

When they realized who was left, they fled to their homes, terrified. Of all the captains to have to live with—thundering Boanerges and that horrendous Captain Conviction!

No one slept that night. Now their only thought was of their own unworthiness. They saw themselves for the first time, rebellious traitors deserving death; they knew that whatever Emmanuel chose to do with them was only right and just. It was the first honest and realistic thought they had ever had, but it was a hard thought to sleep with.

A few days later, the worst possible thing happened; Willbewill and Lord Understanding and Mr. Conscience were taken by Boanerges and locked up in prison. It was the Prince's order. And it was a devastating blow to Mansoul. These three bunglers were the only guides left, and inept as they were, they were certainly better than nothing. With them out of circulation and—who could tell—executed? Horrors.

It would be but the beginning of the end of the town of Mansoul. It would no longer be a question of *whether* they would die, but *how?*

Even so, they drew up a petition to send to Emmanuel, and sent it by a Mr. Desires-Awake. They gave him instructions and wished him a thousand good speeds and waited in a state of numb despair for him to return. When he did, one look at his face and they knew the news was not good. A huge crowd followed him to the prison where Will and Understanding and Conscience were being held.

"I gave him the petition—" he said.

They waited, silent.

"And he turned away. I fancied he might be weeping. But when he turned back to me his face was an enigma; I could not read it."

"But what did he *say?*" they wanted to know, impatient.

"He said he would consider it."

"And?"

"That's all. I was dismissed."

"Doesn't look *too* bad," ventured Understanding.

"Betokens evil!" moaned Will.

"Death!" bellowed Conscience.

The conflicting rumors spread like fire, for different townfolk heard different fragments of the conversation, but the prevailing rumor was "Death!"

It was several days before they recovered sufficiently to do some rational thinking; they decided to send another petition. Some were for sending it by a Mr. Good-Deed, but in a rare moment of insight, Mr. Conscience perceived that the messenger might cancel out the theme of the petition. "I can hear the prince asking him his name," said Conscience, "and I can hear him answer, 'Old Good-Deed,' and I can hear the prince say, 'Ay! is old Good-Deed yet alive in Mansoul? Then let old Good-Deed save you from your distresses.' " It was sound advice, sound advice indeed.

In the end, Mr. Desires-Awake was again elected for the job. Now Mr. Desires-Awake was a man of humble background, and not being as smart or as cultured as the others, he had the audacity of the untutored and untrained—the audacity to suggest that his equally humble and untutored neighbor, Mr. Wet-Eyes go with him to see the prince. This flew in the face of all their thinking, for displays of emotionalism were not entirely to their liking; indeed some held that it was vulgar to even laugh in public. Weeping was an abomination.

All in all, it seemed a highly unlikely twosome for a successful venture, but Mansoul was desperate, so the pair of them went off on their errand loaded with instructions to not, by word or carriage, give any offense to the prince.

They were gone endlessly, it seemed—every moment dragged and no one could eat or sleep. The crowds were waiting for them upon their return but the two would speak to no one but the prisoners. Everyone flocked around the prison and strained to hear. "What did he say?" they wanted to know.

"He said that Diabolus had rebelled against his father and him in the very beginning, thinking to make himself a king and prince. For that he was banished to the pit. Then he offered himself to us—and we chose him over Shaddai. We chose a liar and a murderer for our prince," began Desires-Awake. Everyone was silent, waiting.

"Then he said that his father sent us a powerful army headed by his great captains and we shut them out and fought them and fought for Diabolus against them," Desires-Awake went on. "Then he came to us himself. And as we treated his servants so we treated their lord. We stood up in hostile manner against him, we shut our gates against him, we turned a deaf ear against him and resisted him as long as we could."

There was moaning now, and some tears.

"Then he made a conquest of us. Of all this he reminded us," said Desires-Awake.

Silence.

"Then he said, 'Did you cry to me for mercy so long as you had hopes that you might prevail against me? But now that I have taken the town, you cry; but why did you not cry before, when the white flag of my mercy and the red flag of justice were sent up? Now that I have defeated your Diabolus you come to me for favor; but why did you not help me against him?' "

Silence, utter silence; there was no answer.

"Yet he said that he would, even so, consider the petition and answer it in a way that would glorify himself," said Desires-Awake.

Mr. Wet-Eyes gave a great sigh.

At this point they were all of them struck into their dumps and could not tell what to say. Fear also possessed them in a marvelous manner, and death seemed to sit upon some of their eyebrows.

Finally a man named Mr. Inquisitive elbowed his way to the front of the crowd. "Have you told every whit?" he demanded. "Could there be something you forgot? Think, man, think!"

Mr. Desires-Awake paused for a moment. Then, reluctantly he turned directly to the three prisoners. "It is you who must face the prince and answer his questions," he said. "The prince wants Captain Boanerges and Captain Conviction to bring the three of you to his pavilion tomorrow—"

"This was the thing that I feared!" cried Mr. Conscience.

"—and Captain Judgment and Captain Execution should take charge of the castle and town till they hear further from him," finished Desires-Awake lamely.

"We can never face him!" wailed Lord Understanding.

"By tomorrow before the sun goes down we shall be tumbled out of the world!" bellowed Willbewill, limping about his cell.

Then with one voice they set up a cry that reached up to the heavens. And they prepared themselves to die. All Mansoul concluded that it was only a matter of time.

The town spent that night in mourning and sackcloth and ashes.


What a sad procession the prisoners made next morning, Captain Conviction bringing up the rear. The townfolk of Mansoul showed themselves upon the wall, all clad in mourning weeds, to watch them go.

As they got to the pavilion, the prince had ascended a throne of state and sent for them to be brought in. When they faced him they fell to the ground.

"Bid the prisoners stand upon their feet," he said to Captain Boanerges. And they stood trembling before him.

His burning look demanded nothing less than complete honesty.

88

"Are you the men who used to be the servants of my father, Shaddai?" he said.

"Yes, Lord."

"And you suffered yourselves to be corrupted by Diabolus?"

"We did more than suffer it. We chose him, Lord, of our own mind."

"Would you have been content to continue under his tyranny for as long as you lived?"

"Yes, Lord, yes," they answered, "for his ways were pleasing to our flesh and we were grown alien to a better state."

"And you did not want me to get the victory over you?"

It was hard to answer. "No, Lord, we did not," they said at last.

"What punishment do you think you deserve at my hand?"

"Death, Lord."

"Have you nothing to say for yourselves?"

"Nothing, Lord. You are just; we have sinned."

"Here, then, is my judgment," he said. "Because I have paid the debt of your sin to my father, I have power from him to pardon you."

They waited, hardly daring to breathe.

"And I do pardon you," he said, "I pardon you and forgive you completely."

*Pardon?*

It was so sudden, it was so glorious, it was so great, it was so *big* that they were not able to stand up under it. They fell down at his feet and cried out, "Blessed be the glory of the Lord!"

Emmanuel put his everlasting arms about them and kissed them and commanded them to rise. Then he stripped them of their mourning clothes and put chains of gold about their necks and bracelets on their arms. And he gave them a parchment which was a general pardon and told them to go tell Mansoul what had happened. And they left his pavilion having received what they'd never dared hope for. They possessed that which was beyond all their dreams.

Emmanuel called Captain Faith and commanded that he and some of his officers should march before these noble men of Mansoul, with colors flying.

And the orders for Faith to deliver to Captain Judgment and Captain Execution? Out, out, out! Yes, they were commanded to withdraw from Mansoul and return to the prince. Mansoul was delivered from the terror of the captains of Shaddai!

The dickering, the bargaining, the resisting, were over. Mansoul had faced reality at last.

Mansoul was saved.

HE PRISONERS WERE COMING BACK! WHAT A DAY! THE TOWNFOLK OF MANSOUL LOOKED FROM THE WALLS IN WONDER. THE prisoners had gone to the camp in black; they were coming back to town in white. They'd gone in chains and ropes; they were coming back in chains of gold. They'd gone in fetters; they were coming back with confident strides. They'd gone expecting death; they were coming back with assurance of life. They'd gone with heavy hearts; they were coming back with Captain Faith and with flying colors!

The poor and tottering town of Mansoul gave such a shout as made the captains in the prince's army leap at the sound. And who could blame them for shouting? For it was as if their dead were come to life again. It was like a resurrection, and the feeling spread through the whole town.

When the officers marched in the Ear-gate they were greeted with "Welcome, welcome!" And "How did it go?" And "How will it be with us?" And the officers answered, "Glad tidings! Good tidings of good, and of great joy to poor Mansoul!"

It was Mr. Conscience who put it in one word: Pardon. "PARDON, PARDON, PARDON for Mansoul!" And they shouted until the earth rang. Oh the joy of pardon! He told them to meet in the marketplace in the morning to hear their general pardon read, and they went on their ways rejoicing. What a change in the countenance of the town! No one could sleep that night for joy. From every home were sounds of singing and making merry and telling and retelling the wondrous tale. And they thought, "More of this tomorrow!" It was almost too much to contain. So the night passed.

What a sunrise! What a morning! What a day!

It was the most glorious sunrise Mansoul had ever known. The crowd was in the market square early, eagerly waiting when the officers arrived. And the officers were dressed in the same glory the prince had put on them the day before. The whole street was brightened with their glory. Then the recorder beckoned with his hand for silence and read the pardon with a loud voice. But when he came to these words, "The Lord, the Lord God, merciful and gracious, pardoning iniquity, transgressions and sins—" his voice was drowned in the townfolk's cheering; they could not help leaping for joy.

After the pardon was read, they ran up and down the walls of the town and shouted, "Let Emmanuel live forever!"

Then all the trumpets in Emmanuel's camp were sounded in the distance, and all the colors displayed. The captains showed themselves in all their harness and the soldiers shouted for joy. Even Captain Faith could not keep out of it, though he was in the castle. He showed himself on top of one of the towers and blew his trumpet.

Then the people cleared the center of the market square and the new army of the prince displayed drills and feats of war. They marched, they countermarched, they opened to the right and the left; they divided and subdivided; they closed, they wheeled, made good their front and rear with their right and left wings, and twenty formations more—and then were all as they were originally! The drills ended in a mighty parade, down the main street, trumpets blowing, colors high. It continued out of the town, and on to the camp of the prince. And the town came nigh and touched the top of his golden scepter, and said, "Oh that Emmanuel would dwell with us, that his battering rams and slings would be set for the defense of Mansoul. For we have room for thee, we have room for thy men, we have room for thy weapons of war. Come, Emmanuel, and thou shalt be king in Mansoul forever. Govern us according to the desire of thy soul. And we will become thy servants, and thy laws shall be our directions."

And so he came, clad in his golden armor, riding in his golden chariot, and accompanied by his captains and thousands of his soldiers. The streets were strewn with flowers and boughs; the casements, the windows, the balconies, the tops of the houses, and the city walls were filled with persons of all sorts to behold how their town was to be filled with good. There was music everywhere. The officials and the elders of Mansoul met him to salute him with a thousand welcomes, and walked ahead of his golden chariot all the way to the castle. Captain Faith came out to meet him and to inform him that the castle was cleaned and ready. The cobwebs were gone, the dust bunnies were gone, the dirt was gone, and everything was polished and cleansed and shining. So Captain Faith conducted the prince and his mighty captains and men of war into the castle in the very heart of Mansoul.

Prince Emmanuel had come home.

It was love such as they had never experienced or dreamed of before. No other love had ever been like it; no other love ever would be again.

They thought they never should have enough of Prince Emmanuel. His person, his actions, his words were so pleasing, so desirable to them. It amounted to a craving for his presence. They asked him to walk in the streets and visit the homes often. "For," they said, "your presence, your looks, your smiles, your words are the life and the strength and the sinews of Mansoul." And they wanted continuous and easy access to him in his castle, too. So Emmanuel commanded that the gates should stand open at all times that they might see his doings, as well as the fortifications of the castle and the royal mansion house of the prince.

Emmanuel had the attention of the whole town. The people were completely absorbed in him, so that when he spoke they shut up their mouths and quelled their wandering thoughts and listened. It was their delight to imitate him. To be with him was to satisfy hunger, to be away from him was to be hungry again.

There were special feast days, too. Emmanuel would make a feast for them in his castle and invite them to come and partake of his banquet. What a spread it was! All manner of luscious food—not food that grew in the fields of Mansoul nor in the whole kingdom of Universe. It was food that came from his father's court—dish after strange and wonderful dish he would set before them and they were commanded to eat freely. With each new dish they would whisper among themselves, "What is it? What is it?" for they did not know what to call it. So Mansoul did eat the food that was peculiar to the court. They ate and they were filled. And there was music all the while, played by masters of the songs that were sung at the court of Shaddai.

But the feasting was not all. Afterward, Emmanuel entertained them with riddles of secrets drawn up by his father's Lord High Secretary—riddles concerning Emmanuel and his father, Shaddai. There were no riddles like them in any kingdom. They saw what they never saw before; they never knew such rarities could be couched in such ordinary words. They discovered that many simple things that had meant nothing to them before were really pictures of King Shaddai himself and his son, Prince Emmanuel, and about their dealings with Mansoul. They would consider the riddle, then look on his blessed face and cry, *"You're* the lamb! *You're* the sacrifice! *You're* the rock! *You're* the door! *You're* the way!"* And on and on, there seemed to be no end to the treasures. They were again transported with joy, they were drowned in wonderment, when they saw and understood the mysteries Emmanuel opened to them. They returned home with gifts— precious jewels, gold chains and dainties.

And when they were home and in their most retired places they could not help but sing of him. Yea, so taken were they now with their prince that they would sing of him in their sleep.

There were practical things to do too. Remodeling, for one. And that meant building up and tearing down. For the town had to be put in a condition that would be pleasing to the prince, useful to them, and secure against invasion. Mansoul had to be made strong within and without, against its enemies. Emmanuel gave the orders, and how they scurried about to do his bidding!

New towers! They put on workmen in shifts around the clock and built the towers strong and tall and mounted great slings on them, ordered from Shaddai's court.

A new weapon! Its purpose was to throw stones from the castle, out at Mouth-gate. They installed it with joy, for it was a weapon to be reckoned with; it could not be resisted. Its power was beyond belief—and it was called Intercessor. It was committed to the care of the brave Captain Faith.

The seal of Diabolus? "Down," said Emmanuel, and they fell over each other to obey. In a frenzy of activity they tore it down and beat it into pieces. What to do with the debris? Out, out! They threw it on a dungheap outside the city wall, glad to be rid of it. And in its place they put up the great seal of Shaddai along with the seal of Emmanuel upon the castle gates.

The three strongholds Diabolus had built? "All three must go," said Emmanuel, and a thousand sprang into action as one man. They whacked away until the Hold of Defiance was in shambles and the Midnight-Hold was demolished and the Sweet-sin Hold was a heap of rubbish. They had a time of it too, for these holds were large and sturdy, but they kept at the cumbersome job until at last, sweating and tugging, they carted the timber and the iron and the junk and the dirt that was left, outside the town.

While this was being done, Emmanuel called the three greatest offenders, the three former prisoners—

"Understanding," he said, "I wish to restore you to your former office."

"Yes, Lord."

"And I wish you to build yourself a palace, but this time let it be a palace built like a tower for defense. You will build it near Eye-gate. And you will read in the *Revelation of Mysteries* all the days of your life that you might know how to perform the duties of your office. And Conscience—"

"Yes, Lord."

"You will no longer be recorder for the town. I am making Mr. Knowledge the recorder in your stead."

"Yes, Lord."

"Not out of any contempt for you. Rather, I have something else planned for you. I shall tell you about it when the time comes. And, Will—"

"Yes, Lord."

"I am giving you the care of the gates, the wall, and the towers of Mansoul. I charge you to withstand all attacks made by the enemy, and I will provide you the strength to do so. And I commission you to apprehend and bring to justice all Diabolonians still lurking here."

"Yes, Lord."

"Yours is a great responsibility."

"Yes, Lord, yes. But I believe I am equal to it—with your help, Lord."

"You will be glad to know that some of the worst Diabolonian offenders have already been put into custody and are to go on trial. Some of them are ones Will has already apprehended."

Understanding and Willbewill and Conscience looked at their lord; they were aglow with this new intimacy. It was hard to comprehend, almost too wonderful to believe. They had gone to Emmanuel in fetters, condemned to death. First there was the pardon. Then the robes of praise and chains of gold and the triumphant march back into town. Then the fellowship, the feasts, the songs, the riddles and revelations, the treasures, the special secret gifts and dainties. Then the work of tearing down strongholds and old symbols and putting up new ones. And now this.

What a long way they had come together!

"The trial is set for the very near future," said the prince.

"We'll be there, Lord," they said.

# TRIAL OF THE DIABOLONIANS

HE LAST BIT OF JUNK AND RUBBISH FROM THE STRONGHOLDS OF DE-FIANCE, MIDNIGHT AND SWEET-SIN HAD BEEN HAULED OUT OF TOWN, AND now the Diabolonians in custody were to be hauled into court.

The word spread throughout Mansoul.

On the morning of the trial, the courtroom was buzzing with excitement. Everyone who could possibly squeeze in was there. Crowds outside waited for any word, any rumor, any shred of news that might get out by word of mouth, or waft out on the air.

The principals in the courtroom drama were of every type: famous, infamous, valiant, nefarious, notorious, and every shade in between.

The jury—

Mr. Belief, Mr. True-Heart, Mr. Upright, Mr. Hate-Bad, Mr. Love-God, Mr. See-Truth, Mr. Heavenly-Mind, Mr. Moderate, Mr. Thankful, Mr. Good-Work, Mr. Zeal-For-God, Mr. Humble—

The witnesses—

Mr. Know-All, Mr. Tell-True, Mr. Hate-Lies—with Lord Willbewill and his assistants standing by if they should be needed.

The court—

Lord Mayor Understanding, the recorder, Mr. Knowledge and their assistants were on the bench.

The town clerk—Mr. Do-Right.

And the prisoners! What a haul!

The two ex-mayors of Mansoul, Mr. Unbelief and Lord Lustings, and the ex-recorder, Mr. Forget-Good!

Then there were some burgesses and aldermen who had been apprehended by the now valiant Lord Willbewill and their antics promised to make the trial a dramatic one—Mr. Atheism, Mr. Hard-Heart, Mr. False-Peace, Mr. No-Truth, Mr. Pitiless, Mr. Haughty—

Ah yes, it promised to be quite a day.

The court was called to order and the clerk got down to business immediately. "Set Atheism to the bar, jailer," he said.

And the long day began.

"Atheism," read the clerk, "you are here indicted by the name of Atheism an intruder upon the town of Mansoul for that you have perniciously taught and maintained that there is no God this you have done against the glory of the king and the safety of Mansoul. Are you guilty of this indictment or not?" he read.

"Not guilty," said Atheism coolly, with an air of amusement.

"Call Mr. Know-All, Mr. Tell-True, Mr. Hate-Lies, to the court," chanted the crier.

There was a bit of a hubbub as the witnesses were brought

forth. But things quieted down again as they were sworn.

"You, witnesses for the king," said the clerk, "look upon the prisoner. Do you recognize him? Mr. Know-All?"

"Yes," said Know-All, "we know him. He has been a very pestilent fellow in Mansoul."

"You are sure you know him?"

"Oh yes, my lord. I've been with him too often not to know him. He's a Diabolonian, the son of a Diabolonian. I knew his grandfather and his father."

"He's been charged with teaching that there is no God," said the clerk. "What do you say to this?"

"He and I were once in Villain's Lane together and at that time he talked briskly of many opinions. He said then that there was no God. But he said he could profess to believe in one and be very religious if it were expedient."

"You're sure of this?" asked the clerk.

"Upon my oath," said Know-All.

The clerk turned to the next witness. "Mr. Tell-True?"

"I used to be a great companion of his—I repent of that now. But I've often heard him say he believed there was neither God, angel, nor spirit. He used to be quite vehement about it."

"Do you know much about him?"

"I know he's a Diabolonian. His father's name was Never-Be-Good and he had more children than this Atheism."

"And?"

"I have no more to say."

The clerk turned to Mr. Hate-Lies. "Look at the prisoner," he said, "do you recognize him?"

"My lord," said Hate-Lies, "this Atheism is one of the

worst wretches ever to come out from under a rock. Yes, I've heard him say there is no God, no world to come, no sin, nor punishment hereafter.''

''Where?''

''Where, M'Lord?''

''Where did you hear him say these things?''

''Oh. At Rascal's-lane-end, at the house in which Mr. Impiety lived.''

''Set the prisoner by, jailer,'' said the clerk, ''and set Lord Lustings to the bar.''

Atheism and Lustings passed each other without a glance. Atheism did not look quite so amused. The clerk was reading again.

''Lord Lustings you are here indicted by the name of Lustings an intruder upon the town of Mansoul for that you have devilishly and traitorously taught by practice and filthy words that it is lawful and profitable to indulge carnal desire and that you have not nor ever will deny yourself of any sinful delight as long as your name is Lustings. How do you say? Are you guilty of this indictment or not?''

''M'Lord,'' said Lustings, settling himself, and he hung on to the word, caressing it with mock obsequiousness that was more patronizing than a patronizing air would have been. ''I am a man of high birth and have been accustomed to pleasures and pastimes of greatness. I am not used to being snubbed for my doings but have followed my will as if it were law. And it seems strange to me that I should this day be—''

''We are not concerned with your self-esteem; we are concerned with an indictment preferred against you. Are you guilty or not?''

''—that I should be called into question—''

102

"Will you answer the court?"

"Not guilty." This, with mock patience.

"Crier, call upon the witnesses to stand forth and give their evidence."

The witnesses stood, and the clerk turned to Know-All. "Mr. Know-All, look at the prisoner at the bar. Do you recognize him?"

"Yes, M'Lord, I know him."

"What is his name?"

"His name is Lustings. He was the son of one Beastly, and his mother bare him in Flesh Street; she was one Evil-Concupiscence's daughter. I knew them all."

"You have heard the indictment; what do you say? Is he guilty or not guilty?"

"M'Lord, he has, as he says, been a great man indeed, and greater in wickedness than by pedigree—"

"But what do you know of his particular actions, and especially with reference to his indictment?"

"I know him to be a liar, an unclean person, a lawbreaker. I know him to be guilty of an abundance of evils."

"Where did he commit his wickednesses—in private corners or—"

"All over town, my lord."

The other witnesses verified this and added to it. The clerk turned again to Lustings.

"Lord Lustings, do you hear what these gentlemen say?"

Lord Lustings' voice was as smooth as cream. "I was ever of the opinion that the happiest life that a man could live on earth was to keep himself back from nothing that he desired," he said. "I have lived in the love of my notions all my days. Nor was I ever so churlish as to keep the knowledge of these pleasures from others.''

The court interrupted. ''He has condemned himself; set him by, jailer, and set the next prisoner to the bar.''

Mr. Forget-Good was brought, and the clerk began his reading.

''Mr. Forget-Good you are here indicted by the name of Forget-Good an intruder upon the town of Mansoul for that you when the affairs of the town were in your hand utterly forgot to serve them in what was good and fell in with the tyrant Diabolus against Shaddai against his captains to the dishonor of Shaddai the breach of his law and the endangering of the destruction of the town of Mansoul. What do you say to this indictment? Are you guilty or not guilty?'' the clerk intoned.

Forget-Good leaned forward and spread his hands in a gesture of mock despair.

''Gentlemen, *Gentle*men,'' he said, ''and at this time my judges—I stand accused of several crimes according to my indictment. But I pray you to attribute my forgetfulness to my age and not to my willfulness—''

Understanding nudged Conscience. ''He's going to be quite coy about it,'' he whispered.

Conscience nodded.

''Does the court wish to speak?'' said the clerk.

Conscience shook his head.

''Proceed,'' he said.

''—to the craziness of my brain and not to the carelessness of my mind—'' continued Forget-Good, ''and then I hope I may be excused from great punishment, though I admit I am guilty.''

"Forget-Good, Forget-Good," said Understanding, "Your forgetfulness of good was not simply of frailty but of purpose—"

"But I could not keep virtuous things in my mind."

"You loathed to keep virtuous things in your mind."

"No! I could not retain—"

"What was *bad* you could retain; what was good you could not abide to think of. Don't use your age and craziness of mind to cloak your knavery. But let us hear what the witnesses have to say."

"Mr. Hate-Lies?" prompted the clerk.

"My lord, I have heard Forget-Good say he could not abide to think of goodness for as much as a quarter of an hour."

"Where?"

"My lord?"

"Where did you hear him say so?"

"In All-base Lane at a house next door to the sign of the Conscience-seared-with-a-hot-iron."

"Thank you," said the clerk. "Mr. Know-All?"

"My lord, I know this man well. His father's name was Love-Naught, a Diabolonian. I have often heard him say he counted the very thoughts of goodness a burden and a crashing bore," said Know-All. "In Flesh Lane, right opposite the church," he added in anticipation of the question.

"Gentlemen, you have heard the testimony," said the court. "Next prisoner, please."

"Mr. Hard-Heart," read the clerk when the prisoner was brought. "You are here indicted by the name of Hard-Heart an intruder upon the town of Mansoul for that you did most desperately and wickedly keep Mansoul from remorse and sorrow and penitence all the time of its rebellion against King Shaddai. What do you say to this indictment? Are you guilty or not guilty?''

"My lord," said Hard-Heart, "I never knew what remorse or sorrow meant in all my life. I don't care for any man. I can't be pierced with their griefs. Their groans leave me cold. When I do mischief, when I wrong someone, to me it is music!''

"Nice chap," whispered Understanding, "to have around the house.'' Aloud he said, "He has convicted himself. Set him by, jailer. Set Mr. False-Peace to the bar.''

There was a murmur throughout the court. False-Peace was a master of double-talk; what would he come up with? The clerk was droning on: "Mr. False-Peace you are here indicted by the name of False-Peace an intruder upon the town of Mansoul for that you wickedly and satanically kept the town of Mansoul in a false groundless and dangerous peace during its rebellion to the dishonor of King Shaddai the transgression of his law and the great damage of the town. What do you say? Are you guilty of this indictment or not?'' The clerk's steady tone made the courtroom pay all the more attention to his meaning.

"Gentlemen," began False-Peace. His voice was soft with a hint of a lisp and his countenance was lit up with the psuedo benignity of bad religious art. "I acknowledge that my name is Mr. Peace; but that my name is False-Peace I utterly deny.'' He sighed, adjusted his robes and went on. "I was always a man who loved to live in quiet; and what I loved I naturally assumed others loved also.''

Naturally, thought Understanding, but he kept his face straight.

106

Mr. False-Peace went on. "So when I saw any of my neighbors laboring under a disquieted mind I sought to help them. I just have a sweet temper."

Oh *no*, thought Conscience.

"When Mansoul declined the ways of Shaddai and afterwards some of them began to have disquieting thoughts I tried to quiet them again," False-Peace went on. "When the town was afraid of destruction I merely said it would not come. I have the virtuous temper of a peacemaker, that's all. If a peacemaker be a good man then let me be recognized as a man who does not deserve this inhuman treatment. Grant me my liberty and the license to sue my accusers for damages."

"This is monstrous," whispered Conscience.

"Don't fret," whispered Understanding, "Mr. Do-Right will do right."

As if on cue, the clerk whispered to the crier to make a proclamation.

"Hear Ye!" called out the crier, "Forasmuch as the prisoner denied his name to be that name mentioned in the indictment, the court requires that if there be any in this place that can give information to the court of the right name of the prisoner he should come forth at this time."

Two men rose, and necks craned to see as they came forward and information was buzzed about and relayed from place to place; their names were Mr. Search-Truth and Mr. Vouch-Truth. Mr. Search-Truth took the stand first.

"My lord, I—"

"Hold!" interrupted the court, "give him his oath."

So they swore him in and he proceeded.

"My lord," he began, "I've known this man from a child. I knew his father, Mr. Flatterer. His mother's maiden name was Miss Sooth-Up. I used to play with him when we were children though I was older than he. When his mother called him from play she used to say, 'False-Peace, False-Peace, come home quick, or I'll come fetch you.' "

There was murmuring among the spectators.

"Go on," said the clerk.

"Well I remember him when he was a baby. His mother used to sit with him in the doorway and play with him in her arms and she'd say, 'My little False-Peace! My pretty False-Peace!'—"

There were titters now.

"—'Oh my sweet rogue, False-Peace! Oh! my little bird, False-Peace!' "

And laughter.

"And, 'How I do love my child!' "

Now, the gavel. Search-Truth was asked to step down. Vouch-Truth was sworn in and testified that he remembered when Mr. False-Peace would be angry with those who called him anything else *but* False-Peace, back in the days when he was a great man and the Diabolonians were in power in Mansoul.

Finally the court addressed the prisoner. "Mr. False-Peace, you have denied that your name is False-Peace, but these witnesses have sworn that you have often responded to that name. As to your plea: it is quite beside the point of your indictment. You are not charged for evil-doing because you are a man of peace, but because you kept Mansoul in apostasy and rebellion against King Shaddai in a *false, lying,* and *damnable* peace. Your plea is that you've been called the wrong name; this plea does not cancel your indictment."

"But—" False-Peace stiffened.

"Hold! We'll be fair."

False-Peace sank back again.

"Let's get to the facts of your indictment. Clerk, question the witnesses."

"Mr. Know-All?" said the clerk.

"My lord, this man has made it his business to keep Mansoul quiet in the midst of its lewdness and turmoils. He has said in my hearing, 'Come, come, let us fly from trouble on any grounds and let us be for a quiet and peaceable life; so what if it does *not* have a good foundation?' "

"Come, Mr. Hate-Lies, what have you to say?" said the clerk.

"My lord, I have heard him say that peace with unrighteousness is better than trouble with truth."

"Where did you hear him say this?"

"In Folly-Yard at the house of Mr. Simple, next door to the sign of the Self-Deceiver. He must have said it twenty times if he said it once—"

"We may spare further witness; this evidence is plain and full. Set him by, jailer, and send Mr. No-Truth to the bar."

False-Peace was led off, still protesting with loud ruffling words. There was quite a hubbub before the court was quiet enough to get to Mr. No-Truth.

"Mr. No-Truth you are here indicted by the name of No-Truth an intruder upon the town of Mansoul for that you have set yourself to deface and spoil all the remainders of the law and the seal of Shaddai in Mansoul after its apostasy from its king to Diabolus. What do you say? Are you guilty of this indictment or not?"

"Not guilty, my lord."

The witnesses were called.

"My lord," said Know-All, "this man pulled down the great seal of Shaddai. Also he rent and tore and caused to be destroyed all that he could of the remainders of the law of the king, even whatever he could lay his hands on."

"Who saw him do this?"

"I did, with my own eyes. But so did many others. This was not done by stealth or in a corner but in open view of all. He chose to do it publicly. He delighted in doing it."

The clerk turned to the prisoner. "Mr. No-Truth, how could you have the effrontery to plead not guilty when you were so manifestly the doer of all this wickedness?"

No-Truth looked surprised and a bit affronted. "Sir," he said, "I thought I had to say *something*. And as my name is, so I speak. It's always proved successful before. How did I know? Naturally I thought if I spoke no truth I might come out ahead. It's a lifetime habit, so to speak."

There was a low groan among the spectators. The clerk told the jailer to set him by, and called Mr. Pitiless to the stand.

"Mr. Pitiless you are here indicted by the name of Pitiless an intruder upon the town of Mansoul for that you showed no compassion to Mansoul and would not let it grieve when it had apostatized from its legitimate king but turned its mind away from thoughts that might have led it to repentance. What do you say to this indictment? Guilty or not guilty?"

"Not guilty of pitilessness; my dear sir, all I did was to cheer up. You see my name is not Pitiless, but Cheer-Up, and I could not stand to see Mansoul melancholy."

"How! You too deny your name? Witnesses!"

They came at once and Know-All spoke first: "My lord, his name is Pitiless. It's on his birth certificate and all his legal papers. But these Diabolonians love to change their names; Mr. Covetousness calls himself Good-Husbandry; Mr. Pride can, when it's convenient, call himself Mr. Neat, and so on. All of them are good at it."

"Mr. Tell-True?"

"His name is Pitiless, all right. I've known him from a child. He's done all the wickedness stated in his indictment. But there's a cult of them not acquainted with the danger of damning so they call all those melancholy who have serious thoughts about it."

"Set him by, jailer. Mr. Haughty to the bar," ordered the clerk. "Mr. Haughty you are here indicted by the name of Haughty an intruder upon the town of Mansoul for that you devilishly taught the town of Mansoul to snub the summons given it by Shaddai's captains and to speak contemptuously against Shaddai. How say you? Are you guilty of this indictment or not?"

"Gentlemen, I have always been a man of courage and valor and I'm not used to hanging down my head like a bulrush—"

The courtroom exploded with laughter.

"*Order!*"

There was a sudden silence. The clerk turned to the court.

Conscience spoke; his voice was low and even. He punctuated each word. "You are indicted because you used your pretended valor to draw the town of Mansoul into acts of rebellion. *This* is the crime you are charged with. Is this understood?"

Mr. Haughty did not answer.

"Set him by, jailer," the clerk said, "and send Mr. Unbelief to the bar."

There was a scuffle in the prisoners' section and everyone strained to see what the fuss was about. It was Mr. Unbelief. His face was contorted with hatred, his eyes were glowing with rage. Clearly, he would not fawn or pretend or defend himself. He would die hard.

"Mr. Unbelief you are here indicted by the name of Unbelief an intruder upon the town of Mansoul for that you have feloniously and wickedly while you were an officer in Mansoul resisted the captains of King Shaddai when they came and demanded possession of Mansoul; yea you defied the name forces and cause of the King and stirred up and encouraged the town of Mansoul to resist said force of the King. What do you say to this indictment? Are you guilty of it or not?"

"I do not know Shaddai," Unbelief shouted, starting toward the gentlemen on the bench. "I do not, cannot acknowledge him!" he went on, "I love my old prince!"

"This man is incorrigible—" began the court, but Unbelief would not stop.

"Yes I possessed the minds of the people of Mansoul to do their utmost to resist strangers and foreigners—"

"Hold him!"

"—and I would possess them again given the chance—"

"Order in the court!"

"—nor will I change my opinion for fear of trouble from you—though you have the power at present—"

Several officers jumped on him; he struggled wildly like someone gone mad. "At the *present*—!" he shrieked.

The noise from the gavel could not drown the howl of rage. It took several minutes for the hubbub to die down. At last the courtroom was quiet again.

"This man, as you see, is incorrigible," repeated the court. "He is for maintaining his villainies by stoutness of words, and his rebellion with impudent confidence. Set him by, jailer."

What ignominy, to be set aside with such calm contempt, what humiliation! Unbelief's eyes bulged, his face was a grimace of utter hatred. They dragged him from the courtroom.

Yes, he would die hard.

"Gentlemen of the jury, who shall speak for you?"

"Our foreman, my lord."

"You, the gentlemen of the jury, being impaneled for our lord the king to serve here in a matter of life and death, have heard the evidence regarding the activities of each of these prisoners at the bar. What say you? Are they guilty as charged, or are they not guilty?"

"Guilty, my lord."

"Look to your prisoners, jailer."

This was done late in the morning and in the afternoon they received the sentence of death according to the law.

The prisoners were duly executed according to the law. That is how an official report would have read. But it was not as simple as that. These Diabolonians were brought to die, but *by the hand of Mansoul*. "That I may see," said Emmanuel, "your willingness to keep my word and do my commandments, and that I might bless Mansoul in this effort."

Though it seemed like a valiant effort on the part of the town, and brave and very spiritual in the book of Mansoul's life, these pages were not as heroic as they might have read. Actually they were a comedy of errors on Mansoul's part.

The first humiliation came before the execution even started. Unbelief had the poor taste to escape and nearly undo Mansoul's spiritual smugness all in one fell swoop.

"Alarm the town! Alarm the town! Guard the gates!" The cry went out and rang in every corner. In dismay the inhabitants heard it and in panic they scurried in all directions asking each other how this dreadful thing could possibly have happened, just when they had seemed so on top of it all. Of course an order went out from Conscience and Lord Will-bewill and a thorough search was made, but the culprit could not be found in all the town of Mansoul. All that could be gathered was that he had lurked awhile about the outside of the town, and that here and there, one or another had a glimpse of him as he made his escape. One or two even affirmed that they saw him outside the town going at quite a clip over the plain. There was even one, a Mr. Did-See, who thought he saw him meet with Diabolus off in a distance just upon Hell-gate Hill. Whatever the reports, the awful face was that in the interim betwixt the sentence and the time of execution, he had broken prison and made his escape. And Mr. True-Man the jailer was in a heavy taking because Unbelief was, undoubtedly, the worst of all the gang.

The second humiliation came when the prisoners were brought to the place of execution. It would be hard to believe and harder to admit what troublesome work Mansoul had of it to put them to death; for, knowing that they must die, the rascals resisted mightily, so much so that the men of Mansoul were forced to cry out for help to their captains and men of war. The captains—Faith and Good-Hope and Love and Guileless and Patience—tried valiantly, but in the end, it was the Lord High Secretary who rose up and gave a hand to the executioners so they could put the struggling prisoners to death. So they executed the Diabolonians that had been a plague, a grief, and an offense to the town of Mansoul.

The town was serene again. The Diabolonians were dead, and Unbelief was gone.

But Unbelief had not been put to death.

FTER THE EXECUTION, EMMANUEL
CAME DOWN TO SEE AND TO VISIT AND
TO COMFORT MANSOUL. HE WAS
PLEASED, HE SAID, FOR BY THIS ACT
they had proved to him that they wanted to observe his laws,
that they had respect for his honor. And he continued to turn
their government, their lives, upside down.

To complete the government shake-up, he commissioned
Captain Experience as a replacement for the officers lost.
When this news got out, the hearts of the townsmen were
transported with joy, for he was one of their very own, born
and bred in the town. He had for his lieutenant one Mr.
Skillful and the officer who carried his colors was Mr. Mem-
ory. True, he was a young man, but he was comely, articulate
and very successful in his undertakings.

And then things began to happen; it was as if "all things
had become new," or certainly they were in the process of
becoming.

*First, a new charter!*

Yes, the prince laid the old one by and said, "That which
is getting old and decaying is ready to vanish away." He

declared that Mansoul should now have another, and it should be a better one, a new one. And it was! It gave them full and everlasting forgiveness of all wrongs done against Shaddai, Emmanuel, their neighbors and themselves. It gave them the law and Emmanuel's testament. It gave them a portion of the very grace that dwelt in Emmanuel's heart. It gave them free access to Emmanuel in his palace at all seasons. And it gave them the full power and authority to seek out and destroy any Diabolonians who might be found straggling in or about the town.

Mr. Knowledge the recorder read the new charter in the marketplace; then it was engraved on the doors of the castle in letters of gold so they might always have it in their view. As this was being done, the bells rang, the minstrels played, the people rejoiced, the captains shouted, the silver trumpets sounded and the colors waved in the wind. Any Diabolonians still in town were glad to go hide their heads, for they looked like them that had been long dead.

*Then, a new ministry!*

"For," said the prince, "unless you have teachers and guides, you will not be able to know and do the will of my father." At this news the whole town came running, so happy were they with their new prince, and so eager to do his pleasure.

"I will establish two among you," he said, "one, a native of Mansoul. You know him well. Your old recorder, Mr. Conscience."

Old Conscience stepped forward; he looked in fine fettle, well exercised and glowing with health. They looked at him with new respect. "He will teach you and guide you in so far as he is capable," Emmanuel went on, "I am making him your minister, to instruct you in domestic matters of morals and government.

"The other is from my father's court—my father's own Lord High Secretary—dictator of all his laws; a person as skilled in all mysteries and knowledge of mysteries as is my father or me. Indeed he is one with us in nature, he is the very spirit of my father and me."

The Lord High Secretary stepped forth. A great hush came over the crowd. For he was the one who sat at the table during the love feasts and explained the riddles and unraveled the mysteries. And he was the one who had stepped forth and put his hands on the hands of the executioners and given them the power to kill the hard-to-die Diabolonians!

"And this is he," said the prince, "who must be your chief teacher. For it is he and he only who can teach you clearly in all high and supernatural things. It is he who can bring lost things to your remembrance. It is he who can put life and vigor into your heart. And it is he who can help you draw up petitions to my father and me. Without him you can do nothing."

The hush remained over the crowd; they were soberly impressed.

"Do nothing without his advice. He is your chief teacher, your highest guide. Make your requests to us, my father and me, through him. He is your source of power. Take heed how you treat him; do not grieve him."

Emmanuel turned back to Conscience. "You must confine yourself to civic and natural duties. You must not attempt to presume to be a revealer of mysteries that are kept close in the bosom of Shaddai. No one can reveal them but my father's secretary only. So be his scholar and a learner, even as the rest of Mansoul. Go to *him* for information and knowledge.

"Teach Mansoul," he concluded, "but if they will not hearken, teach them with whips and chastisements."

*And new robes!*

"And now, I have something for you to set you apart," he said. And he called his attendants and they brought forth out of his treasury beautiful robes, glistening white. "These are my livery—a badge of honor—by which you will be known as mine. Wear them daily so that all will know you are set apart, belonging to me. And keep them clean, for if they be soiled it is a dishonor to me. Tuck them up to keep them from the ground; don't let them drag in the dirt. But if you should sully them, come to me quickly through the Lord High Secretary and tell me about it, so that I may cleanse them again."

Next he charged them to treat their captains well; to love them, nourish them, encourage them, for they were guards against the enemy. And if they should at any time be sick or weak and so not able to perform their offices, not to slight them nor despise them, but rather strengthen them and encourage them. He had the captains stand forth—Faith, Good-Hope, Love, Guileless and Patience. "If these captains be weak," he said, "then Mansoul cannot be strong; if they be strong, then Mansoul cannot be weak. Your safety lies in their health."

And then he cautioned them to beware of the Diabolonians still lurking in the town, ready to spring in an unguarded moment. "Hearken diligently to me," he said, "they are implacable. They study and plot to attempt to bring you to destruction. They are the avowed friends of Diabolus. They used to lodge with their prince in the castle when Unbelief was the mayor of Mansoul. But since my coming, they have scurried to the back streets and to the walls, and have made themselves dens and caves and holes and strongholds therein. You can never utterly rid yourselves of them. But you *can* be diligent and quit you like men; observe their holds, find out their haunts, assault them, make no peace with them."

Then he called some of the lingering Diabolonians by name. "The Lord Adultery, the Lord Murder, the Lord Anger, the Lord Lasciviousness, the Lord Deceit, the Lord Evil-Eye, Mr. Drunkenness, Mr. Reveling, Mr. Idolatry, Mr. Witchcraft, Mr. Variance, Mr. Emulation, Mr. Wrath, Mr. Strife, Mr. Sedition, Mr. Heresy—they are skulkers in Mansoul!"

"But how shall we know them?" they cried.

"Look well into the laws of Shaddai," he answered, "and there you will find their descriptions and their characteristics. If you let them run about the town they will poison your captains and turn you into a barren waste. Heed their descriptions well, for some of them will appear to be very religious. They will do you more mischief, if you do not watch, than you can dream of.

"Do not let them deceive you," Emmanuel finished, "they are always in hiding. Apprehend them whenever you find them; put them to death.

"Watch and pray," he said as he dismissed them. He said it softly and yet it seemed to thunder and echo and reecho and stay in the very air.

It did not seem possible that things could get any better,

but they did. For these were the golden days. Mansoul was like the signet upon Emmanuel's right hand. A town redeemed from the power of Diabolus! A town Shaddai valued and Emmanuel loved to dwell in! The wonder of it! Teachers, guides, captains, white robes—it was more than they'd ever dared dream of. Now there was unbroken fellowship. There was not a day that the elders of Mansoul neglected to come to him or he to them. They would walk and talk together of all the great things that he had done and was yet to do for Mansoul. This would he often do with Lord Mayor Understanding, and Lord Willbewill and Mr. Conscience and the new recorder, Mr. Knowledge. How they hung on his every word!

They wanted to be together continually; every day was a feast day now. He spread delicacies before them in abundance, and he never sent them away empty. Either they must have a ring, a gold chain, a bracelet, a white stone, or something; so dear was Mansoul to him, so lovely was Mansoul in his eyes.

And as if all these things were not enough, he put Mr. God's-Peace over them as governor of the town.

Yes these were the golden days. There were no jars, no chiding, no unfaithful doings in all the town of Mansoul; everyone kept to his own job and observed his duties, so that nothing was to be found but harmony and joy and good health. The influence of Mr. God's-Peace was in the air like a sweet perfume; the friendship of the Lord High Secretary gave them joy and power that they had never known before.

And this lasted all that summer.

ATCH AND PRAY," THE PRINCE HAD SAID. "THERE ARE DIABOLONIANS STILL HERE. DO NOT DECEIVE YOUR-SELVES."

Well, no. The last thing they wanted to do was deceive themselves, spoil all this happiness and prosperity. But it was difficult to know—for, quite frankly, there were such inconsistencies and Mansoul was so mixed up by nature that sometimes it was difficult to tell who was a real enemy and who was not.

Mr. Carnal-Security hurried out of his house and started up the street. He was a very well-dressed gentleman, a little on the portly side with the florid face and commodious stomach of the self-indulgent and the liberal-minded. He walked with a quick sure stride, his head high and confident, and he had an aura of success and prosperity about him that made those who met him on the street nod their heads in deference and all who knew him socially or in business treated him with a certain awe. He was highly conceited, but at the same time, very charming and winsome, two diverse traits that somehow seemed to live together comfortably within him.

He walked to the market square and began to cross it, calling out jovially to those about their day's business. He was an imposing and important figure, fearless and sure of himself. Indeed he came by these traits quite naturally. For long ago, when Diabolus had first taken possession of the town of Mansoul he'd brought with him a great number of Diabolonians. That dread day when he had called out, "Go in quietly," it was not only the war lords and officers and soldiers that had swarmed in, but a host of Diabolonians had also invaded and had been quartered throughout the town. They had not only married among themselves and bred, but intermarried with Mansoulians and produced half-breeds, and the weird combinations of these offspring were legion.

Among those who had swarmed in that dreadful day, there was one whose name was Mr. Self-Conceit, and he was as notable and brisk a man as any who possessed Mansoul in those days. Diabolus, with his keen eye for perceiving sharp recruits to do his work, had noticed this chap almost at once, and had given him jobs of greater and greater importance. These jobs he executed with greater efficiency than any from the deepest dens could have done, and he'd risen in the ranks until he was placed in a position next to Lord Willbewill himself. Naturally Willbewill had been greatly pleased with Self-Conceit in those days, and it was only a matter of time before the young upstart was courting Will's daughter, Lady Fear-Nothing. Everybody had been agreeable to the match including Lady Fear-Nothing herself, and in due time they were married. Baby Carnal-Security had been the result of this match. Carnal-Security had grown in stature and craft, and had learned his tricks from those in authority over him, both by inheritance and example. He took after both his father and his mother; he was self-conceited, he feared nothing. But he had picked up a few other tricks besides.

He learned, for one thing, to spurn the weak and align himself with the strong, and to shift sides if it were expedient. So, although he was a great doer for Diabolus during the rebellion by encouraging Mansoul to resist the king's forces, when he saw that the town was taken and converted to the use of the glorious Prince Emmanuel and Diabolus was rousted out with contempt and scorn, he slyly wheeled about and, as he had served Diabolus against the prince, he now feigned to serve the prince against Diabolus.

He had done very well, too. There was no news, no doctrine, no talk of alteration afoot but that Mr. Carnal-Security would be at the head or tail of it. He made it his business to acquire a smattering of the things of Emmanuel—caught them by the tail, so to speak, and, armed with this, he ventured into the company of the townsmen and chatted with them and picked up various connections and friendships.

He was, to be vulgar, a backslapper. He said things people wanted to hear. He spoke in glowing terms of the power and strength of Mansoul. He chatted amiably in the clubs of its fortifications and weapons. He flattered lavishly the captains and officers at their many luncheons. "Yes *sir,*" he was wont to say, "you are certainly *going* places. Impregnable! Nothing can trip you up now. Nothing!" All of which made him the most delightful company, and the townsmen were tickled and quite taken with his discourses. And so they went, from talking to feasting and from feasting to sporting, until at last Mansoul was dancing after his pipe and growing almost as carnally secure as himself.

On this particular morning he was in fine spirits; he stopped at the edge of a little park in the market square, picked a flower and arranged it in his buttonhole. He thought of his good looks and many talents and fine position and especially of the good impression he would make on Lord Understanding and Willbewill and Conscience. They were meeting for breakfast. He had, he mused, a ring in the nose of everybody who was anybody in Mansoul. Things were looking good, yes, very good indeed.

Lord Willbewill left his house and hurried down the street. He was looking very dapper, feeling very gay and stepping with confidence. He looked prosperous and happy, as indeed he was. Mansoul was still in a golden era. Things had never been brighter. His affairs both at home and in his work were going first-rate. He thought of his keen mind and his ability to make decisions and the marvelous shape he had been keeping himself in. He passed the castle, hesitated a moment, wondered if he should go in. He was to meet his colleagues and Mr. Carnal-Security for breakfast and he was already a bit late. He consulted his timepiece briefly, frowned slightly, and hurried on. He noticed a smudge on the side of his robe, stopped and tried to wipe it off with his sleeve, and failing, folded the material over and walked on, calling out a hearty greeting to someone who hailed him from across the street. Then he quickened his pace again; there was more elasticity in his step than ever before and the smudge on his robe was hardly discernible.

Lord Understanding hurried along the street toward the market square where he had an appointment with Will and Conscience and Mr. Carnal-Security. He was walking briskly, his feet hardly touching the ground. He radiated confidence, and no wonder, for his powers of discernment had seemed exceedingly sharp of late, in spite of the fact that he'd had little time for research. He had taken a speed-reading course to help him in this area, and although he was too busy to put it into practice, he did find that it came in handy in getting through the word of Shaddai quickly. Of course it militated against meditation on choice words and passages, but in these busy times one did what one could. At any rate he had never seemed in better health, and the respect he commanded among his peers was flattering and gratifying. Mr. Carnal-Security was a delightful chap, he thought, as he breezed past the castle without a sideward glance. It was nice to be appreciated. He continued on his way, already forming in his mind some sharp comments to make upon current topics of the day that might be brought up during the breakfast conversation. Some trash blew across his path and he walked through it without knowing, for he was glancing upward. The sky seemed quite murky; a cloud had come over the sun. As he neared the market square he remembered that he should have stopped in at the castle. It was too late now, he thought, and continued on his way. The sky was darker now but he did not notice.

Mr. Conscience hurried toward the market square. There was a spring in his step and he felt remarkably clearheaded considering that he had been up late the night before. Mr.

Carnal-Security's parties were fashionable and smart and stimulating, but it was hard to get up in the morning. He glanced nervously in the direction of the castle as he passed by. He knew he should drop in but there really wasn't time; he'd be late for breakfast with Mr. Carnal-Security. As he hurried on he noticed a slight pain in the region of his middle; no, it was more like a pang. He decided not to fuss or worry about it. Wasn't Mansoul in better shape than it had ever been? Mansoul was, as Mr. Carnal-Security had said so often, impregnable. Such talent, such beauty, such strength! His robe caught on a bush by the wayside and tore a bit but he did not feel it. He hurried on; it was beginning to sprinkle.

Prince Emmanuel waited for the officials of Mansoul to come to his castle to partake of the love feast he had prepared for them. But they did not come. They had not come for quite some time. Nor had they noticed whether or not he went to visit them. He had prepared the love feasts regularly but they had neglected them; their delight in the feasts was gone. They had stopped going to the Lord High Secretary, too, for counsel and teaching. They made their own decisions now. They did not need the prince. They no longer delighted in him quite so fully because they delighted more in the power and the gifts he had given them. They did not wait for his love or his counsels but were headstrong and confident in themselves, believing they were strong and invincible and secure and beyond all reach of the foe and that this state would be unalterable forever. Twice he had sent the Lord High Secretary to warn them that they were on dangerous ground, but both times they had been at dinner in Mr. Carnal-

Security's parlor and did not have time to reason.

Emmanuel looked at the feast and the dainties and the precious gifts and thought of Mansoul and bemoaned them and condoled their state with the Lord High Secretary. "Oh that my people had hearkened unto me, and that Mansoul had walked in my ways," he said. "I would have fed them with the finest of the wheat; and with honey out of the rock would I have sustained them."

### NOTICE

This is to serve notice that Mr. God's-Peace is laying down his commission and will for the present act no longer as governor of the town of Mansoul.

Breakfast grew into brunch, the company was so jolly, the conversation so stimulating; Mr. Carnal-Security was indeed a delightful host. It was on the way home that Conscience and Willbewill and Understanding saw the notice in the market square. It had blown loose from one nail; a brisk breeze had come up and the corner was flapping wildly. Conscience held it down so they could all read it, then they looked at each other in dismay. It was disquieting news. They decided to go to the castle at once and make amends.

As they neared the gate, bits of rubble and leaves from uncleaned streets blew across their paths. Will caught his foot in the hem of his robe at one juncture and ripped it a bit; they pinned up the tear and hurried on.

At the castle gate they knocked and waited. No one came. They knocked again. Strange. The prince used to run to meet them halfway and embrace them. They knocked again. No sound, nothing. The breeze had grown into a cold wind. They grew impatient. They compared timepieces and considered their busy schedules. They decided to go on about their business.

As they left, the rain came suddenly, whipping their robes about them and lashing against the castle windows. It whipped across the market square too, in sheets, tearing at the notice of Mr. God's-Peace's resignation. The notice flapped until it finally gave way and went scurrying across the empty square.

It was stopped at the edge by a bush and there it stayed, impaled on a thorn, and the cold rain soaked it through.

# A PROPHET AT THE PARTY

HE STORM CLEARED AND THE DAYS THAT FOLLOWED WERE HAPPY ONES. MANSOUL WAS DOING VERY WELL. THE TOWNFOLK GREW STRONGER AND more self-sufficient as time went by. They had never before really been aware of their gifts and talents; Mr. Carnal-Security made them realize that they were many. Mr. God's-Peace was not missed as much as they had thought he might be, nor the feasts with the prince, for that matter. They were growing strong and tough on Carnal-Security's doctrine, and as the weeks grew into months, more and more confident of their charm and ability. Self-confidence was a heady business; it gave a glow to the cheek and a spring to the step; they congratulated themselves and each other on their radiant appearance. Meanwhile Mr. Carnal-Security kept the town entertained with lavish banquets. They grew larger and more lavish as he added more of Mansoul's gentry to his guest list, until he had almost everybody who was anybody dancing attendance. But he was ever on the lookout for other influential townfolk, to bring them under his spell.

One night, a few months after God's-Peace had laid down his commission, old Carnal-Security gave a huge party to which all the powers-that-be were invited. This particular night he had invited a Mr. Godly-Fear, hoping by the influence of the jolly company to lull him into smug and comfortable complacency.

The guests arrived, the mansion was ablaze with light, the table was groaning under the weight of all kinds of delicacies, and the huge rooms were abuzz with excitement and high spirits. Everyone was bustling with self-importance and merry with self-appreciation—everyone but Mr. Godly-Fear. He sat apart, like a stranger. He did not eat or drink; he would not be drawn into the conversation or the laughter. Mr. Carnal-Security watched him with growing uneasiness. He was apparently not going to succumb easily; clearly he needed a bit of a boost. Mr. Carnal-Security leaned toward him with one of his most disarming smiles.

"Mr. Godly-Fear, are you not well? I beg your pardon but you seem to be ill. Here. Here is a cordial of Mr. Forget-Good's making."

"Sir," said Godly-Fear discreetly, "I thank you for all things courteous and civil, but—"

"It's delightful. A dram of this will make you bonny and blithe, and so make you more fit for us feasting companions."

"—thank you, but I do not care for your cordial."

"Oh come, come! It will take the weight off your mind."

"I do have something on my mind, sir. I would like to have a word with the chiefs of Mansoul." And he scraped his chair back and got to his feet. "You—elders, chiefs, yes and natives of Mansoul—it is strange to see you so merry when Mansoul is in such danger."

Mr. Carnal-Security was horrified. "Mr. Godly-Fear," he whispered, "you really look ill. You want sleep, good sir, no doubt. If you want to retire—"

"No I don't want to retire. Sir, if you were not completely destitute of heart you could not do what you have done to Mansoul."

Now the room was very quiet. Everyone was straining to hear.

Carnal-Security started to rise. "Mr. Godly-Fear, what are you talking about?"

"You know well enough! You have stripped Mansoul of her strength and left her wide open to the enemy."

"I've done nothing of the sort," Carnal-Security was on his feet now.

"Then I'll explain," said Godly-Fear. "From the time that my lords of Mansoul and you, sir, grew so great—"

"A feast is made for mirth; why then do you now, to your shame and our embarrassment, break out into such a passionate, melancholy language when you should eat, drink and be mer—"

"From that time—"

"If you will, please—lie down and take a nap and meanwhile *we* will be merry—"

"*From that time,* the strength of Mansoul has been offended—"

"Fie! Fie! Mr. Godly-Fear, fie!"

"You have weakened its towers, you have weakened its gates, you have spoiled the locks and bars."

Mr. Carnal-Security threw out his hands in a conciliatory gesture. He spoke softly with mock patience. "Mr. Godly-Fear, what's the matter with you? Why are you so timid? I'm on your side. Only you're for doubting and I'm for being confident."

"Confident of what?"

"Mansoul is impregnable."

"Mansoul *was* impregnable—with a *proviso*— complete dependence on Emmanuel. Mansoul's strength was not in its towers—it was in *Emmanuel*. And that strength is gone—"

"My dear sir, if you please—"

"No—don't interrupt me. I will not be silent. It isn't time to flatter or be silent." He turned to the others. "Do you question that your strength is gone?" he flung at them. They were gaping at him foolishly in unbelief. "Yes—I see the question in your faces. I'll answer your question with a question. Where is Prince Emmanuel?"

There was not a sound in the room.

"Well?" he said.

Silence.

"When did you see him last? When did you hear from him or taste any of his dainty bits? When did you sit at his table for a love feast? When have you talked with him, really talked with him? When have you *sought* him?" His voice fell to a whisper. "When have you seen his face?"

The effect was stunning. They looked as if they'd been dealt a blow.

"You cannot answer," he thundered, "because he's gone! You were too busy for him and he's *gone!*" He gestured with contempt toward Carnal-Security. "You are now feasting with this Diabolonian monster, but *he is not*

133

*your prince!* Emmanuel is gone without so much as acquainting the nobles of Mansoul with his going. If that is not a sign of his anger then I am not acquainted with the methods of godliness.''

Carnal-Security recovered himself. "Mr. Godly-Fear, will you never shake off your timidity? Are you afraid of being sparrow-blasted?''

"Emmanuel did not withdraw all at once,'' Godly-Fear continued as if he had not been interrupted. "He kept himself close but more retired at first; his speech was not as familiar, nor as pleasant as it had been.''

Carnal-Security appealed to the gentlemen at the table. "Who has hurt you?'' he asked.

"My lords and gentlemen,'' continued Godly-Fear, "your gradual declining from him provoked him gradually to depart from you, hoping you would be made sensible by his actions and be renewed by humbling yourselves.''

"Who has hurt you?'' Carnal-Security insisted.

"But when he saw that none would take these fearful signs of his anger to heart, he went away from this place; and this I saw with my own eyes.''

*"Who has hurt you?''* Carnal-Security said again. No one was listening to him, no one at all.

"Oh, Conscience—Will—Understanding—'' Godly-Fear looked at them sadly, "you have been feasting with the one who has driven your lord away.''

He gestured toward Carnal-Security, but he was still looking at them, "While you boast, your strength is gone.''

They stared back at him incredulously.

"Your lord is gone,'' he said quietly, "and you don't even know when he left.''

134

Silence.

Then Mr. Conscience got slowly to his feet. He was trembling so he could scarcely stand. He spoke to the others but he was still staring at Mr. Godly-Fear. "Indeed, my brothers," he said, "I'm afraid that what he says is true."

"I like not such dumpish doings," muttered Carnal-Security and stalked out of the room. No one glanced his way.

"I, for my part," Conscience went on, "have not seen my prince for a long long time. I've been—so busy." His voice shook; they waited for him to go on. "I cannot remember the day, nor can I answer Mr. Godly-Fear's question. I'm afraid it's all up with us."

Mr. Godly-Fear nodded his head toward the door where Carnal-Security had just left. "With your prince, no enemy from without could have made a prey of you; yet, since you have sinned against him, your enemies from within have been too hard for you to withstand."

Mr. Conscience looked as if he would fall down dead at the table. He sank back into his seat. Godly-Fear looked around the banquet table and searched the pale faces of the other elders and officers. Not one of them could meet his eyes. "Since without him you can do nothing and he is departed from you, turn your feast into a sigh and your mirth into lamentation," he said quietly.

No one answered. For a long time.

"How did we miss it?" said Willbewill, finally. "It seems so obvious now, how did we miss it?"

"It seemed to happen in an instant," said Conscience. "Our world came crashing down."

"No, it's been happening for a long time," said Understanding. "It came to a climax in an instant."

"We've been thriving on Carnal-Security's doctrine," said Willbewill.

"We've been drunk on his doctrine," said Understanding.

"The words of our prince come very hot into my mind," said Conscience.

"It's about time," said Godly-Fear.

"Do you remember what he told us to do to Diabolonians who would rise to delude us?" Conscience went on.

Everyone was silent for a moment. Then it began, first as muttering, then louder, then sporadic shouts, then one great shout that filled the mansion.

"Burn him! Burn Carnal-Security and his house with him! *Burn him! Burn himmmmmmmmmmmm!*"

HESE WERE DAYS OF CLOUDS AND OF THICK DARKNESS IN MANSOUL. THEY HAD BEEN DARK AND CLOUDY EVER SINCE MR. GODLY-FEAR'S OUTBURST that awful night at the banquet. After that night, all Mansoul was awake. For it was true. Emmanuel had left Mansoul. He had departed from them as they had turned from him— gradually. Now they saw how foolish they had been; they began to comprehend what the company and prattle of Mr. Carnal-Security had done and what a desperate plight his swaggering words had brought to Mansoul.

In their first outburst of repentance they had burned Mr. Carnal-Security and his mansion with him.

Then they began to look for Emmanuel. They sought him but they found him not.

First they thought of the Lord High Secretary. Of course, he could tell them where Emmanuel was and how they might direct a petition to him. He knew everything. He would give them power and wisdom and intelligence with the prince. All

137

they had to do was knock on the door of the prince's abode in the heart of the castle.

But he would not see them.

Then they thought of sermons. Of course. That would do it. They assembled and listened to Conscience preach, and oh how he did thunder and lighten the day! His text was from the prophet Jonah, "They that observe lying vanities forsake their own mercy." And he preached with such authority that when the sermon was over they were scarcely able to go to their homes or betake themselves to their employment the week after. They were sermon-smitten.

But it did no lasting good.

Then they tried fasting, to humble themselves for being so wicked against the great Shaddai and his son.

But it was no use.

Then they got Boanerges, the great man himself, to preach. His text was "Cut it down; why cumbereth it the ground?" and a very smart sermon he made upon the place. First he showed that the problem was that the fig tree was barren; then he showed that the sentence was utter desolation. Then he showed by whose authority this sentence was pronounced and it was none other than Shaddai himself. And he was so pertinent in his application that poor Mansoul trembled anew and it kept awake those who were roused by Conscience's sermon the week before.

But it did not help.

Then they drew up a petition to their offended prince asking that he in his favor and grace would turn again to them, and sent it to the court of Shaddai by Lord Understanding.

But the gates were closed.

Then they counseled with Godly-Fear with mourning and

weeping, and he told them to keep on trying, for it was the way of the wise Shaddai to make men wait and exercise patience. They were the ones who had wronged him; they should try again and again and again and be willing to wait for him to answer. They did.

But it was hard to wait.

They had the good intentions; they had repented with their customary enthusiasm. But after the first burst of fervor was over, the awful truth was they could not hang on. A great weakness swept over the town of Mansoul like an epidemic, and most of the inhabitants were greatly afflicted. The men of war languished, and worse still, the captains! Captain Faith—Good-Hope—Love—Guileless—Patience—all became weak and ill. Oh how many pale faces, weak hands, feeble knees and staggering men were now seen to walk the streets of Mansoul! Some were groaning, some panting, and yonder lay those who were ready to faint.

And their garments! The snow-white robes Emmanuel had given them were in sorry condition; some were rent, some were torn, and some hung so loosely upon them that the next bush they brushed past was ready to pluck them off.

But worst of all their morale was at rock bottom. They would have been an easy prey for enemies lurking within or for invasion from without.


Lord Anger came out of the front door of his apartment. Well, actually he slithered out of a crevice in Mansoul's wall down near Feel-gate. It was a poor excuse for a lodging but he had lived there ever since Prince Emmanuel had taken over the town. And he had managed to make it do while he waited for better days to come back again. Once on the street, he looked both ways to check for possible foes lurking about and, finding none, he pulled his hat down, his cloak collar up, and slithered uptown toward the market square. On his way he stopped by to pick up his old friend Lord Deceit, who came squiggling up from his hold under the wall, in answer to Anger's low whistle. The two of them walked on, talking in undertones and sneaking furtive glances about, their eyes darting into the nearest crack at the thought of any opposition. Their vigilance was unnecessary; there was no one around to cause them any trouble.

"Well, M'Lords!"

They started for a moment. But it was only the old and dangerous villain, Mr. Covetousness, standing under a street sign. The three of them chatted a while, then went up the street called Vilehill, toward the den of Mr. Mischief, where the meeting was.

These meetings were usually well attended. There was little excuse for absenteeism; the Diabolonians who met were lively and enthusiastic and in extremely good health. Lord Adultery, Lord Murder, Lord Lasciviousness, Lord Evil-Eye, Lord Blasphemy and a host of others. Some of them had come with Diabolus when he invaded and took the town; some of them were there by reason of mixed marriages. All of them had their holds and dens and lurking places in, under, or about the wall of the town.

The good prince had granted a commission to Lord Will-bewill and others, to seek, take, secure and destroy any or all of the rascals that they could lay hands on. And, with their characteristic enthusiasm they had started out with much fuss and ceremony to root out every lurking Diabolonian, to kill him without mercy. But before they'd well-started, complacency had set in.

The Diabolonians had things well calculated. They simply hid in their cracks when the squeeze play was on, ventured forth when the pressure was off, comforted each other and admonished each other to be not weary in evildoing, and waited for a time to strike.

The time to strike was now.

The light from the sputtering candle in Mischief's den sent their shadows shooting up the sides of the wall and halfway across the ceiling as they crouched on the floor. They were a weird lot.

"We could offer ourselves as servants," said Lord Lasciviousness. "Get into their homes. Corrupt them from within."

"Not at this time," said Lord Murder. "Mansoul is in a kind of a rage right now, weak as it is. Carnal-Security just ensnared them; once bitten, twice shy. I veto that."

"What do you suggest, then?" said Mr. Mischief.

"That we be wise as foxes. They're under orders to kill us as we are. Dead, we can do them no harm. While we live, we may. I'm for playing safe."

"And what is safe?" said Mischief.

"I'm not sure," said Murder. So the meeting was thrown open for discussion. In the end they decided to write to Diabolus and ask his advice in the matter.


A few days later, Mr. Profane hurried over the plains,

whistling his favorite dirge in F minor. The letter that had been composed in the den of Mischief was safely tucked away beneath his cloak. He was still whistling when he finally came to Hell-gate Hill. He knocked at the brazen gates for entrance. After much horrible squeaking and grinding, the gate was opened and Cerberus, the porter, stuck his head out.

"Why Mr. Profane—what brings you here?" Cerberus' face was contorted with glee.

"May I see his Lordship at once?" said Profane impatiently.

"Why yes. Come in, come in, come in. Welcome back, Mr. Profane." Suddenly Profane let out with a horrible howl. "Oops, sorry, didn't mean to close that gate on your hand. Come right this way, sir, his lordship is in the main den." And he led the way through tortuous passageways until—

"Tidings, M'Lord, from Mansoul, from your trusty friends in Mansoul," cried Profane—and he and Diabolus fell upon each other, slapping backs and exchanging all the routine greetings of the pit.

"I have a letter here," began Profane when he could disentangle himself. He fished for it, started to hold it aloft, but Diabolus snatched it from his hand.

"Letter?" he cried. "Ahhh. Pardon me, I didn't mean to scratch you when I grabbed it. What have we here?" He ripped it open and began to read, muttering to himself.

"To our great lord, the prince Diabolus, dwelling below in the infernal cave:

"O great father and mighty Prince Diabolus, we the true Diabolonians yet remaining in Mansoul cannot endure the town with content and quiet without you.

"The reason for this letter is that we are not altogether without hope that this town may be yours again—" Diabolus broke off reading.

"Porter! Cerberus! Call Beelzebub, Apollyon, Alecto—all the rest of the rabblement—eh—personnel—from all parts of the den. They'll want to hear this!

" '—*greatly declined'*—Where was I? Oh, yes. Here we are. 'For it is greatly declined from its prince Emmanuel. He has departed and though they send and send—'

"Ah, here you are. Crouch, all of you. You'll be interested in this. Apollyon, Beelzebub, the rest of you—you all know Profane. Emmanuel has left Mansoul. Listen to this: 'Though they send and send and send after him to return to them they cannot prevail nor get good words from him.'

"Now this is good, oh this is good. 'There has been of late great sickness and faintings among them, especially the lords, captains and chief gentry of the place (we only who are Diabolonians by nature are well, lively and strong). All in all, we feel that they lie open to your hand and power.' "

He glanced around to see how they were taking the good news, and satisfied, went back to reading, "If therefore, you wish, with your horrible cunning, to come and attempt to take Mansoul again, send us word and we shall do our utmost to deliver it into your hand. Send us your suggestions in a few words and we are ready to follow your counsel to the hazarding of our lives and all we have.

"Given under our hands the day and date above written, after a close consultation at the house of Mr. Mischief, who yet is alive and hath—"

He did not wait to finish.

"I've been hoping for this, oh I've been hoping for this!

Porter! Have dead-man's bell rung for joy! Without stopping! And loud! I think best in the midst of a lot of noise!''

The bell began to toll, and a horrible noise it made. He listened with satisfaction for a moment. Then he began to pace back and forth. ''Alecto—take this down: 'To our offspring, the high and mighty Diabolonians that yet dwell in Mansoul: We have in our desolate den received, to our highest joy and content, your welcome letter by the hand of our trusty Mr. Profane. And to show how acceptable your tidings are, we had dead-man's bell rung for joy. We rejoice to hear that Mansoul has fallen into a degenerated condition. Its sickness pleases us, as does your health, might and strength. How glad we would be, right horribly beloved, if we could get this town into our clutches again. We are willing to spend our wit, our cunning, our craft, and all hellish inventions in order to do so.

'' 'Here is what we, the trusty princes of the pit, suggest. Pry into and spy out! Pry into and spy out their weaknesses! Then attempt to weaken them more and more. We submit three methods for you to consider: (1) Persuade them to live a vain and loose life, or (2) Tempt them to doubt and despair, or (3) Blow them up by the gunpowder of pride and self-conceit.

'' 'Be always in readiness to make a most hideous assault within when we are ready to storm it without. And now speed you in your project to the utmost power of our gates. This is the wish of your great Diabolus, Mansoul's enemy, and him that trembles when he thinks of judgment to come. All the blessings of the pit be upon you.

'' 'Given at the pit's mouth, by the joint consent of all the princes of darkness, to be sent to the force and power that we have yet remaining in Mansoul, by the hand of Mr. Profane. By me. DIABOLUS.' ''

The Diabolonians all fell upon Profane when he returned to the den of Mischief with the letter.

"And how is our master?"

"And Cerberus, how is he? Old dog of Hell-gate!"

"They are all as well as can be expected, under the circumstances," said Profane. "But they're all so anxious to get back here; our letter was a great encouragement to them. And here's an answer."

They all fell upon the letter then, and nearly tore it to shreds before it could be read. Then they crouched around to decide what should be done.

"The first and most important thing," said Mischief, "is to keep from Mansoul any designs we might contrive against them. Remember, absolute secrecy. Now. Gentlemen, what is your pleasure? Lord Deceit?"

"He has suggested three ways to undo them," Deceit began. "Make them loose and vain, drive them to doubt and despair, blow them up with self-conceit. Now, I think, if we should tempt them to pride, that may do something; if we tempt them to wantonness, that may help. But in my opinion, if we could drive them into desperation, that would knock the nail right on the head."

They all nodded in satisfaction.

"For," Deceit went on, "then we should have them question the truth of the love of their prince toward them. Then they stop sending those petitions. And *then* they conclude that as long as they're not getting anywhere, they might as well give up."

They nodded again, "But how? How do we do this?"

"You remember," Deceit answered, "when you suggested that we hire out as servants and I said no."

"Yes you said no," they remembered.

"Well now I say yes," he said, "But *disguised*. Some of us are more suited to a project like this than others. I suggest three to start with. Mr. Covetousness, Lord Lasciviousness and Lord Anger."

He thought a moment. They waited in silence.

"Mr. Covetousness as—Prudent-Thrifty."

"How subtle!"

"Lord Lasciviousness as—let's see—how about Harmless-Mirth?"

"How clever!"

"And Lord Anger as Good-Zeal."

"Genius! Bravo!"

And so it was decided. And then the letters began to fly back and forth between Mr. Mischief's den and the pit.


## MEMO

◆————◆

*FROM: Underground in Mansoul*
*TO: Diabolus*

*The lords of looseness send to the great high Diabolus from our dens, caves, holds and strongholds in and about the wall of the town of Mansoul, greetings:*

*Our great master, how glad we were when we heard of your*

*readiness to help us forward our design to ruin Mansoul.*

*First, we considered your hellishly cunning suggestions and decided that to drive them to desperation was the best plan of all.*

*Second, we have sent three of our trusty Diabolonians among them disguised, and you will be happy to hear that they had no trouble in getting themselves hired out as servants. They clothed themselves in sheep's-russet, which was as white as were the white robes of the men of Mansoul. As they could speak the language of Mansoul well, when they went to the marketplace and offered themselves for hire they were taken up almost at once; for they asked but little wages and promised to do their masters great service.*

*What they changed their names to is a matter of great mirth; you will never believe how clever we were. Mr. Covetousness called himself by the name of Prudent-Thrifty and was hired by Mr. Mind. Lord Lasciviousness called himself Harmless-Mirth, and it's true he did hang a little in hand and could not get hired as readily as the others because of Lent. But as soon as Lent was over, Lord Willbewill hired him to be both waiting man and lackey. Lord Anger changed his name to Good-Zeal and got hired by Mr. Godly-Fear, but we're sorry to tell you that he did not fool his master for very long. It was, in fact, no time at all before that peevish old gentleman took pepper in the nose and turned the poor chap out of his house. The others are doing very well though and are making their masters almost as wanton as themselves, and we hope to get Lord Anger hired out again soon.*

*We suggest that you come upon the town on a market day when the townspeople are the busiest and the most preoccupied. For it is then that they will feel most secure and least apt to think of invasion. They will also be less able to defend themselves and give you trouble.*

We also suggest that when you attack, you use an army of doubters. For of all the legions that are at your whistle, we think doubters may be the most likely to overcome the town.

Meanwhile we are happy to report that they get sicker and weaker and, all in all, things are looking up. Be assured that we already have a foot in their door; it is only a matter of time.

To the monsters of the infernal cave, from the house of Mr. Mischief in Mansoul, by the hand of Mr. Profane.

# MEMO

*FROM: Diabolus*
*TO: Underground in Mansoul*

*Beloved offspring in the den of Mr. Mischief, greetings:*
We received your letter with great joy; it was good to see Mr. Profane so lively and strong. We can only wish the rest of you are prospering as well as he. With your letter the hollow belly and yawning gorge of the pit gave so loud and hideous a groan that it made the mountains about it totter as if they would fall in pieces.

Your first project in Mansoul is likely to be lucky; if you can succeed in making Mansoul yet more vile and filthy, more power to you. For there is no way to destroy a soul any more successfully. In fact this should be for us a maxim and general rule for all ages; for nothing can make this fail but grace, and we certainly would hope that there will be no grace around to abound for Mansoul.

Whether to fall upon them on a market day because of their preoccupation and cumber in business is a matter for debate. We should consider this carefully, for upon this will turn the whole of what we shall attempt. The success of the entire enterprise depends upon timing; if we do not time our business well our whole project could fail. What if, for instance, they should double their guards on those days? It seems that reason and plain common sense would teach them to do it. Of course the question is whether Mansoul has that much sense. If they are as asleep as you seem to indicate of course any day will do.

Please advise us. Does Mansoul know how bad off it is? Or of our designs? Is it apt to be wary and double its guards?

In haste and impatience, to be sent to the Diabolonians in Mansoul, by the hand of Mr. Profane.

*By Me, DIABOLUS.*

## MEMO

◆ ‥ ◆

FROM: *Underground in Mansoul*
TO: *Diabolus*

Great and high Diabolus, from our dens in Mansoul, greetings:
As far as we can gather, this is at present the condition of the town of Mansoul: (1) They are decayed in their faith and love. (2) Emmanuel their prince has turned his back on them. (3) They have sent and are sending frequent petitions to fetch him again; in fact their messengers are meeting each other going and coming on the road to Shaddai's court. (4) He seems in no hurry to answer their petitions. (5) There does not seem to be much reformation among them.

To mighty Diabolus, from the den of Mischief by the hand of Profane.

# MEMO

FROM: Diabolus
TO: Underground in Mansoul

Friends in Mansoul, in the den of Mr. Mischief:

We are glad to hear they are backward in reformation but we are very much afraid of their petitioning. However, let us not be too discouraged; their looseness of life is a sure sign that there is not much heart in what they do, and without the heart, their petitions will be nothing but words, words, words.

My war lords tell me to advise you to go slowly and remind me that what Carnal-Security did can be done again; two or three Diabolonians, if accepted by Mansoul, can do more harm than an army or a legion that could be sent out by us. So I should tell you to carry on. But this I find very hard to do. My empty paunch is lusting!

To my trusty friends in Mansoul, from the pit, by the hand of Profane.

*By Me, DIABOLUS.*


# MEMO

FROM: Underground in Mansoul
TO: Diabolus

Mighty Diabolus, from the den of Mischief, greetings:

Oh great master, we wait impatiently too. We are still prosecuting your design by using all our power, cunning and skill to draw

150

*Mansoul into more and more sin and wickedness. We shall con-*
*tinue to debauch them so that by the time you attack they will be*
*utterly unable to make resistance.*

*To our lords in the pit, from Mischief's den, by the hand of*
*Profane.*

## MEMO

———————◆———————

*FROM: Diabolus*
*TO: Underground in Mansoul*

*Trusty ones in and about the walls of Mansoul, from the dark and*
*horrible dungeon of the pit, greetings:*

*I know you have been waiting impatiently for our most devilish*
*answer to your venomous and poisonous design against the town of*
*Mansoul. My gaping gorge and yawning paunch are on fire to put*
*your inventions into execution. I am raising, therefore, an army of*
*more than twenty thousand doubters to come against that people,*
*with all the speed I can. You must still use all your power, cunning*
*and skill to draw them into even more sin than they are already.*

*As to the time of our coming upon Mansoul, we as yet have not*
*fully resolved upon that. But when you hear our roaring drum*
*without, your orders are to make the most horrible confusion*
*within. Then Mansoul shall be distressed before and behind and*
*shall not know which way to betake itself for help.*

*My war lords salute you! Cerberus, the dog of hell, wishes to be*
*remembered to you!*

*From our dreadful confines in the pit, by Mr. Profane.*
                              *By Me, DIABOLUS.*

# MEMO

FROM: *Underground in Mansoul*
TO: *Diabolus*

*Great master, Diabolus, from the den of Mischief, greetings:*
*All is well! We are in. The Mansoulians send petitions and regard iniquity in their hearts. They grow weaker. They cry to their king for help and take Diabolonians to their bosoms. The Diabolonians and the Mansoulians walk the streets together. There is no great difference now between them. So come ahead! Things were never better!*

*In haste, from the den of Mischief, by the hand of Profane.*

## DIABOLUS ATTACKS AGAIN

HE CURFEW HAD RUNG IN MANSOUL. THE PEOPLE HAD LONG BEEN IN THEIR HOUSES. THE SHADES WERE DRAWN. THERE WAS NO MOON AND THE STREETS were poorly lighted; most of the streetlamps had been damaged. A chill wind swept the market square and worried the shutters on the castle windows. Sometimes it seemed to be running anxiously through the streets and up the alleys; sometimes it seemed to disintegrate into one big shuddering sob.

The wind caught the robe of the lone figure walking along one of the side streets, now pulling it out behind him, now trying to wrap it around his ankles. He walked on, oblivous to the tug and pull, his glance darting from alley to window to crevice to bush, as if trying to ferret out anything that might be hiding. His face was sharp and intelligent, his eyes inquisitive, and there was an urgency in his steps and manner.

He was out walking because he had not been able to sleep—a malady that had plagued him all his life. "Mr. Prywell," his servants would say, "it is dangerous to take these walks so late at night. Mansoul is so dark and the wind is so chill; you'll catch your death.'' But old Prywell would lie upon his bed, far after everyone else had gone to sleep, unable to close an eye. In the end he would succumb to his restlessness and sneak out to wander the dark streets, to pry. For Prywell was a great lover of Mansoul, and jealous for its well-being. He was always fearing some mischief would befall it, either from Diabolonians within or from some power without. King Shaddai had made him this way; indeed it was the great king himself who planted these thoughts in Prywell's mind.

The next street sign was in darkness, but Prywell knew it by heart. It was Vilehill. He had prowled up that way often. He turned the corner and walked soundlessly past the dark houses. He was nearly past Mischief's house when he saw the long thin shaft of light reflected on the hedge. He stopped, looked, and backed up a few paces. It was coming from a slit in the improvised drape drawn over a basement window. He crawled through the hedge and slithered on his belly up to the window and waited. There was no sound at first. Then he heard the voices inside. Evil voices—bragging, laughing, telling of the plot to weaken Mansoul within—letters flying back and forth between Mansoul and the pit—Diabolonians hiring out as servants under assumed names—seducing, undermining, lying, destroying. And an army—at least twenty thousand strong, led by Diabolus himself—an army of hand-picked doubters—already on the way!

Prywell listened until it was almost dawn. Then he made a run for it across the dangerous lighted space, back to the hedge. He crawled through and sneaked back down Vilehill, keeping to the shadows. After he turned the corner he ran, his footsteps echoing through the empty streets, clear across town until he came to the house of Lord Mayor Understanding. He ran up to the huge front doors and pounded loudly with both fists. It was some time before he heard footsteps inside. Then, after the sound of considerable fussing with locks and bolts and bars on the inside, the door opened a little way and a servant in a nightcap poked his head out.

"Yes?" he said with some annoyance.

"The mayor!" cried Prywell, "I must see the mayor."

"Have you an appointment?" said the servant, gaping stupidly.

"Blast the appointment! No I don't have an appointment. But I *must* see him!" said Prywell.

"But he's barely up yet. And he hasn't had his breakfast," protested the servant.

"Blast his breakfast!" shouted Prywell. "When he hears what I have to tell him he won't want any breakfast!"

The servant opened the door the rest of the way and Prywell dashed into the hallway. The servant started down the hall, shuffling and reluctant.

"It's urgent!" bellowed Prywell. The servant lunged forward as if the words had given him a shove, and hurried toward the stairway.

An hour later, Understanding and the other gentlemen he had hurriedly summoned to the emergency meeting listened with pained faces as Prywell finished his tale.

"A wholesale massacre," said Understanding.

"And we're playing right into their hands," said Conscience.

"At least now we know what we're fighting," said Will. "What shall we do?"

"Plenty," said Conscience, and he stood up. "M'Lord

Mayor, with your permission I'll have the lecture bell rung. I'll speak to the people, and you, Mr. Prywell, you ought to speak to them too; tell them firsthand what you saw, what you heard. And we'll go on from there."

They got busy then with bell cords, notes, messengers and hurried conferences.

"Breakfast, sir?" asked a servant, poking his head in.

"No breakfast," said the mayor.

Already the lecture bell was ringing.


The market square was crowded. The people came tumbling out of their houses in response to the lecture bell, and stood huddled together in the chill wind to hear what Conscience had to say. He told them the enemy, both inside and outside, was plotting their ruin. He painted a vivid and horrible picture of the dispatches flying back and forth between the den of Mr. Mischief and the princes of the pit. He warned them to renew their guard and be watchful. He told them the Diabolonians were just waiting for a market day to catch them unawares. And he told them it was past time for deceiving themselves—it was time to call a spade a spade. They were weak and sick and faint. They were sending petitions to Emmanuel and courting Diabolonians in their midst. It was time to face up to the facts. It was time to clean up. Then he told them of the army of doubters being assembled to march against them, and called on Prywell to substantiate his words.

When they finished speaking the crowd stood absolutely silent for a moment.

Then they wept.

The effort to reform was all-out, very courageous, and pitiful. All gates were locked and guarded. No one was allowed to come or go without being searched. Mr. Prywell was sent on a special secret mission to Hell-gate Hill to spy on the enemy's doings. The patrols polished their buttons and badges and made a house-to-house search for lurking Diabolonians and rooted them out. Those harboring Diabolonians were brought to the market square to make public confession. Some of it was humiliating, for many harboring the culprits were citizens in high office. In the very house of Mr. Mind and in the house of the great Lord Willbewill two of them were found, Prudent-Thrifty, alias Mr. Covetousness, and Harmless-Mirth, alias Lasciviousness. They were committed to custody under Mr. True-Man who handled them so severely they died in prison.

But for the most part the Diabolonians were almost impossible to capture. The captains and elders sought them diligently in dens and caves and holes and crevices, but though they could plainly see their footings and follow their tracks and smell their abodes, the culprits would still slip away, because their ways were so crooked, their holds so strong, and they so quick and nimble to slip from the grasp and take sanctuary until it was safe to come out again.

A day of public confession of faults and fasting was declared. The captains drilled their men in maneuvers and put them back on the proper diet. There were clean-up days and clean-up weeks and rallies and revivals.

They were as ready as they could be, wide awake, braced for action and very very frightened when the report came back from Prywell's intelligence corps. Diabolus was ready to march.

And that old renegade, the worst of the lot who had escaped execution during those first days, was the general of the army!

Old Unbelief!

The people of Mansoul trembled. They were weak and they knew it. They were weak—but now they were awake!

The dreaded army came like a cloud on the horizon at first. Then it took shape. Soldiers—thousands of them—there seemed to be no end to them—coming on inexorably. They were a terrible sight to behold.

*Election-Doubters* under Captain Rage; his colors were red, his standard-bearer was Mr. Destruction and his emblem was a red dragon.

*Vocation-Doubters* under Captain Fury; his colors were pale, his standard-bearer was Mr. Darkness and his emblem was the fiery flying serpent.

*Grace-Doubters* under Captain Damnation; his colors were red, his standard-bearer was Mr. No-Life and his emblem was the black den.

*Faith-Doubters* under Captain Insatiable. His colors were red, his standard-bearer was Mr. Devourer and his emblem the yawning jaws.

*Perseverance-Doubters* under Captain Brimstone. His colors were red, his standard-bearer was Mr. Burning and his emblem was a blue and yellow flame.

*Resurrection-Doubters* under Captain Torment. His colors were pale, his standard-bearer was Mr. Gnaw and his emblem the black worm.

*Salvation-Doubters* under Captain No-Ease. His colors were red, his standard-bearer was Mr. Restless and his emblem the prince of death.

*Glory-Doubters* under Captain Sepulcher. His colors were pale, his standard-bearer was Mr. Corruption and his emblem a skull and dead men's bones.

*Joy-Doubters* under Captain Past-Hope. His colors were red, his standard-bearer was Mr. Despair and his emblem a hot iron and a hard heart.

These were the captains and these were their forces with their standards and their colors and their emblems. Over them were Lord Beelzebub and Lucifer and Legion and Apollyon and Python and Cerberus and Belial. But over them all was *Unbelief.*

And Diabolus was their king.

IABOLUS BEGAN TO PLAY HIS GAME WITH MANSOUL AND TO WORRY IT AS A LION WORRIES ITS PREY. HE WANTED TO MAKE MANSOUL FALL FROM SHEER TERROR.

First there was the streaming of colors, terrifying and dejecting to behold, and the hideous noise of Diabolus' drummer.

Mansoul panicked.

Then there came a furious assault on Ear-gate.

Mansoul recoiled, but recovered and retaliated with stones from Emmanuel's golden slings.

Then Diabolus cast up several mounts and put up banners bearing his own name and the names of the furies of hell.

The captains and soldiers of Mansoul kept up with their barrage and he was forced to retreat. Then both sides dug in for the grim game ahead.

Diabolus commanded the drums to be sounded all night. There was no noise ever heard so terrible and no one could sleep who heard it. Then his drummer beat for a parley.

Mansoul did not answer.

Captain Sepulcher summoned them in the name of Diabolus, to open the gates without further ado and let him enter or they would be swallowed up.

The people of Mansoul made no answer to him. But they looked to the law of Prince Emmanuel, and Understanding studied it intensely until he had found some comfort for them. And they were encouraged.

Then Diabolus approached again for another assault.

They answered him with more stones from Emmanuel's slings, and the sling stones were to him like hornets.

He retreated.

They rang bells for thanksgiving.

Diabolus then turned from threats to sugar-talk. Promises. Promises, the same old ones, repackaged and more clever than ever.

They cried back: "LIAR!"

Thereupon Diabolus fell into a hellish rage, regrouped his captains and made another furious assault. Outside Mansoul all hell broke loose.

Inside Mansoul the defenders mounted their slings, set up their banners, sounded their trumpets and continued fighting back. Meanwhile they slaughtered more resident-Diabolonians.

## CASUALTY LIST OF DIABOLUS

Captain Rage . . . . . . . . . . . . . . . . . . . . . . . . wounded
Captain Cruel . . . . . . . . . . . . . . . . . . . . . . . wounded
Captain Damnation . . . . . . . . . . . . . . made to retreat
Captain Much-Hurt . . . . . . . . . . . . . brains beaten out

161

Captain Anything

Captain Loose-Foot

Captured and
put in irons

## CASUALTY LIST OF MANSOUL

Lord Reason . . . . . . . . . . . . . . . . . . . . . . head wound

Lord Understanding . . . . . . . . . . . . . . . . . eye wound

Mr. Mind . . . . . . . . . . . . . . . . . . . . stomach wound

Mr. Conscience . . . . . . . . . . . . . . . wound near heart

Many underlings wounded

No fatalities

## THE MANSOUL DAILY BULLETIN

### NIGHT SALLY FAILS: CAPTAIN FAITH WOUNDED!

*A sortie of troops from besieged Mansoul attempt-ed a night attack upon the camp of Diabolus. En-couraged by recent victories, Captain Faith, Captain Good-Hope and young Captain Experience led a small hand-picked band into the enemy camp.*

*Diabolus and his men, expertly accustomed to night work, gave them battle and the fighting was heavy. The Prince's captains fought stoutly, inflicted many casualties and caused the army of Diabolus to make a retreat.*

*While pursuing the enemy, Captain Faith stumbled and fell, badly wounded, resulting in disorder among the troops and causing them to retreat. The retreat*

*turned into a rout when Captain Good-Hope and Cap-*
*tain Experience fainted. Diabolus, supposing them to*
*be dead, did an about-face and came upon the Prince's*
*army with hell-fury and cut, wounded and pierced*
*them severely.*

*What through discouragement, disorder and*
*wounds, the men were scarcely able, though they had*
*for their power the three best hands in Mansoul, to get*
*safely into the stronghold again.*

The battle continued.

Diabolus, flushed with victory and encouraged by the indisposition of the three captains, came upon Mansoul again and demanded entrance.

Lord Mayor Understanding replied that he, Diabolus, would have to take Mansoul by force, for as long as Emmanuel was alive they would never yield to another. Lord Willbewill added that they had been turned from darkness to light, from the power of Diabolus to Shaddai, and that though they had sustained losses, they would rather die fighting than give up.

These words were like a balm to Captain Faith's wound.

Willbewill harassed more Diabolonians within the town—Lord Brisk, Lord Opinionated, Lord Carping and Lord Murmur among them. Some were wounded, some sorely maimed, though none were slain outright.

"One more try," said Diabolus. "One more bout. I beat them once, I know I can beat them again."

"Where?" said Beelzebub. "When? How?"

"Feel-gate," said Diabolus. "Night. And now, while

Captain Faith and Good-Hope and Experience are so badly wounded. Never be another chance like this. And how? All-out assault.''

He gave the orders to bend all forces against Feel-gate and attempt to break into town through that. The word he gave to his officers and soldiers was *Operation Hell-fire*. "Let nothing be heard in that town all night," said Diabolus, "but Hell-fire.'' The drummers were also to beat without ceasing and the standard-bearers were to display their colors.

The Mansoulians resisted fiercely, but after Diabolus' army struggled awhile at Feel-gate, he threw it wide open, for those gates were weak and most easily made to yield. He placed Captain Torment and Captain No-Ease there and attempted to press forward, but the prince's captains came down upon them and made his entrance more difficult than he had hoped.

They made what resistance they could. But three of their best and most valiant captains were wounded: Captain Faith, Captain Good-Hope, Captain Experience. The rest had their hands full because of the doubters. They were overpowered. Nor could they keep the enemy out.

"At the last," said Diabolus, "it was their emotions that did them in.''

O THE CASTLE!''
ONCE THE BREACH HAD BEEN MADE
THAT BECAME THE GOAL. THAT WAS
THE ULTIMATE PRIZE. WHOEVER WON
the castle won the fight. For the castle was the prerogative-
royal of the Prince Emmanuel.

The prince's men and their captains got there first.

The enemy spread themselves throughout the rest of the
town, and in every corner could be heard the dreadful roaring
beat of Diabolus' drum and the cry of ''Hell-fire!''

And now did the clouds hang black over Mansoul, now
did Mansoul feel the fruits of sin and the venom that was in
the flattering words of Mr. Carnal-Security.

Diabolus quartered his army in the houses of the gentry.
Conscience's house was filled with them, and Lord Mayor's
castle and Lord Willbewill's abode. And every cottage, every
barn, every hog sty was filled with them. And most of the
culprits were doubters.

They ravaged the town.

These were long dark days. Sin bore fruit and Mansoul
was finding it out the hard way. But they did all they could,

and Diabolus and his men were not at peace for a moment. The captains plagued them with slings from the castle and the townsmen browbeat them when they could. Meanwhile they hid stores and supplies from them; whatever the villains got they got reluctantly and with an ill will. They never did get into the castle though they made repeated attempts for many days. Mr. Godly-Fear was keeper of the castle, and many wished that Godly-Fear had been keeper of *all* of Mansoul.

But the town was divided against itself, and the glory of Mansoul was laid in the dust.

Incredibly, Mansoul wallowed in this state for these two long years, grieving over its miserable condition and the miserable judgment visited upon its people.

Diabolus was getting nippy. "I wish they'd either get worse or better," he kept whining. "This half-way business is about to do me in."

"But we haven't really lost them," his war lords would try to comfort him.

"We don't really have them either," he would snap.

He was captious with his underlings too. His demons and his doubters could do nothing to please him. "Mind you, don't get careless," he would say, "watch what they do to relieve their misery. Drive them to complaining, drive them to quarreling, drive them to drink, drive them to anything but petitions!"

"Yes, master," they would say. They would say it and say it and say it, but he was never comforted.

"If I so much as catch one of them—just *one* of them on his knees—"

Every one would tremble at the very thought.

"Down in the bottomless pit you go!" he would shriek.

"By my own hand. I'll toss you there myself!"

The very thought was enough to send them scattering in all directions looking for cracks.

It was not the thought of petitions that worried him; as long as they were spurious or purely emotional or halfhearted or sporadic he had nothing to fear. It was the thought of petitions sent through the Lord High Secretary and the thought of importunity that made him tremble.

"But Understanding has a bad eye wound," they would comfort him, "and Mr. Mind's stomach wound has him laid up indefinitely. Captain Experience is still wounded. Mr. Conscience—"

"Yes I know," he would moan. "I know, I *know*,"

"And we still have control of Feel-gate," they'd say. "Why are you so downcast?"

It was Mr. Godly-Fear that frightened him, and they knew it. He was almost certain that it would be through Godly-Fear that Mansoul would finally find its way out of darkness.

Diabolus' worst fears came true one gloomy afternoon when the captains and the gentry were shut up in the castle bemoaning their wretched state and, after much fruitless talk, they decided to send Prince Emmanuel one more petition; it had been some time since they'd tried. Mr. Godly-Fear stood up. "The prince never has and never will receive any petition from anyone unless the Lord High Secretary's hand is upon it," he said.

"Why haven't you told us that?" they said.

"I have," he answered quietly. They looked at each other, battered, bandaged, half sick. He had? They did not remember and they were too weak to argue.

"Then we'll draw up one," they said, "and get him to sign it."

"But he will not sign it unless he has a hand in drawing it up," Mr. Godly-Fear said.

They remembered. Of course. Prince Emmanuel himself had told them this—back during the golden days when it seemed nothing could ever go wrong. Was it a thousand years ago?

It was a sad little delegation that visited the Lord High Secretary that gloomy afternoon. Understanding, with a patch over one eye—Captain Experience on crutches—Mr. Conscience in a wheelchair—Willbewill limping badly. The captains were there too—Faith, Good-Hope, Love, Guileless, Patience. And Mr. Mind. And some others. They all looked as if they could use some vitamins. They were a pathetic little band. But a determined little band.

The Lord High Secretary was kind. "What petition is it that you would have me draw up for you?" he said.

"But you know best!" they cried. "You know our condition! How we are degenerated—backslidden from the prince. You know we're at war—that Diabolonians walk our streets with more boldness than our townsmen dare to—"

"I'll draw up a petition for you," he said, "and sign it."

"We are grateful!" they cried. "When shall we call for it?"

"You don't call for it," he answered. "You must be present at the doing of it. Indeed, you must put your desires to it. The hand and the pen shall be mine, but the ink and the paper must be yours; else how can you say it is your petition? Do you see?"

They looked at him. Yes—they understood. The late

168

afternoon sun broke through the clouds and came in from the skylight and spilled over the gloomy room and on his face, and they saw him too, as they'd never really seen him before—as a priceless friend that sticketh closer than a brother. And they poured out their hearts in that petition.

"Forgive us!" they cried out to Emmanuel. "We are discouraged and sick and frightened and brokenhearted. We are surrounded on every side; our own backslidings reprove us; the Diabolonians within our town and on our streets frighten us. We have weakened our captains and they are discouraged and sick and wounded. Lord, our enemies are lively and strong; they vaunt and boast and threaten to part us among them for a booty. They've fallen upon us with thousands of doubters; they are grim looking and terrifying and unmerciful and we cannot tell what to do. Our wisdom is gone and our courage is gone and our strength is gone because you have departed from us, and there is nothing left here but confusion. Take pity upon us, O Lord, take pity upon us and deliver us out of the hands of our enemies!"

They watched him as he wrote, their eyes bleak, their faces desperate. He finished the petition, attached his seal to it and handed it solemnly to Captain Faith. "Out Mouth-gate tonight," he said softly, "and straight to Emmanuel."

Faith nodded. Then they filed out without a word, crutches and wheelchairs and all, and they were helping each other.


Diabolus heard about it the next morning. He stormed through town, across the market square, through the castle gates and up to the castle itself.

"You rebels!" he screamed, shaking his fist at the upper windows. "You miserable stubbornhearted clods! I'll make you leave off petitioning! Are you still bent on petitioning? I'll make you stop!" And he turned to his aides. "The drum!" he bellowed. "Have the drum beat again! Noise! Noise! They can't abide the noise!" He ran a few feet, leaped upon one of the castle walls and faced a group of Diabolonians that had gathered. "These miserable Mansoulians have dared to send to Emmanuel's court for help! This I give you to understand—I command that you distress this town and vex it with your wiles—*brain them!* Mischief! Mischief! Kill their children! Brain their ancients!" He was frothing in a desperate rage. But he knew well who had delivered the petition and he was trembling as he leapt from the wall and dashed back to the castle doors.

"Let us in! Let us in on pain of death! Open the doors!"

Mr. Godly-Fear replied from the other side, "The doors will not be opened—to you or to any who follow after you," he said. "Moreover, Mansoul has suffered for a while, but will be strengthened and made perfect and whole again."

Diabolus looked around quickly at the Diabolonians and turned back to the castle. "Deliver me the men who petitioned against me!"

No answer.

"Especially Captain Faith! Deliver that varlet Faith into my hands and I'll get out of Mansoul—I'll never bother you again! Better one man perish than all of Mansoul be undone!"

"And how long will Mansoul be kept out of the dungeon after we have given up Captain Faith?" Godly-Fear said, "If we lose Faith we lose Mansoul."

Understanding heard them from his quarters. He opened an upper window and stuck his head out. "Tyrant!" he shouted, "let us tell you something: We shall not listen to you. We are resolved to resist you as long as there's one stone left in Mansoul to throw at you. And one man left to throw it!"

"Do you hope? Do you wait? Do you look for help and deliverance?" Diabolus looked incredulous. "*You* have sent to *Emmanuel?* And you think you shall prosper?" He walked a few steps and turned, for maximum force. "But your wickedness sticks too close in your skirts to let innocent prayers come out of your lips, doesn't it? *Doesn't it?*" He waited for that to have effect. Then he began to speak slowly and deliberately, "You will fail in your wish, you will fail in your attempts, for it is not only I, but your *Emmanuel* who is against you." He spoke faster. "It is he who has sent *me* against you to subdue you! He has left you to *me!* For what, then, do you hope? And by what means will you escape?"

There was a dreadful silence.

Then Lord Understanding leaned farther out the window. "Yes we have sinned, but that shall be no help to you," he cried, "for Emmanuel has said it and we believe it: 'And him that cometh to me I will in no wise cast out.' He has also told us that all manner of sin shall be forgiven us. And we believe it! We dare not despair! We look for it! We wait for it! We hope for it! We know it will come!"

Just then Understanding heard the shouts ringing through the corridors of the castle. "Captain Faith has returned! Captain Faith is back!"

He closed the window and wheeled around leaving Diabolus shrieking against the castle doors, his sudden spurt of courage gone.

"He's back from Emmanuel's court—and he has a package!" someone shouted. Understanding started for the door, all the anger leaving him. As he made his way to the Chamber of State he suddenly realized he was almost afraid to hear Faith's report. He was weak with fear and despair. He opened the chamber's door and went in. All of the gentry were waiting. The captain did have a package. "What is the news from the court, captain?" Understanding asked, his eyes filled with tears.

Captain Faith laid his package aside on the table and faced them. Will looked completely broken. Conscience had a look of dogged and stubborn perseverance. Understanding was weeping behind his eye-patch. They all looked weary. And frightened. "Cheer up," said Faith quietly. "You've all been doing well; don't be weary now. Victory is within your grasp. I have something in general to communicate to Mansoul. And some special messages for each of you."

They stared at him, immobile with the shock of relief. He began to take notes from his package.

"Lord Mayor," he said, "you've been bold for your prince in these dark days. Your responsibilities have been great; you've borne up well. Emmanuel is pleased." He handed Understanding a note. Understanding took it soberly; his eyes did not leave the captain's face.

The notes were passed around to the others in silence, and as each opened his, the despair turned to joy and the joy permeated the whole room. But it was a quiet and thoughtful joy. They exchanged their messages with each other. Emmanuel had taken it well that Lord Willbewill had been so faithful in apprehending Diabolonians in Mansoul. He had taken it well that Conscience had performed his office of exhorting and forewarning. That Godly-Fear had recognized Mr. Carnal-Security for what he was. That Mansoul had sent repeated petitions. He had known. He had cared. He had been watching. He had been watching every one of them perform his office. And their feeble efforts *he had taken well*.

"You weep," said Faith, looking from one to the other.

"We weep with joy," said Will. "But it is a cautious joy."

"Cautious?" said Faith. "You have reservations about Prince Emmanuel?"

"I have reservations about myself," said Will. The others nodded.

"I'm on my way to see the Lord High Secretary," said Faith. "I am to be commissioned to manage this war." He looked at Understanding. "It is a war," he said quietly.

No one moved for a moment. Then Faith gathered up the remaining packet of communications and started for the door. They watched in silence. In the doorway he turned, looked at them again. "Trust me," he said. "Put me to work. It *is* a war. And it's not over yet. And we're going to win it."

HAVE TWO THINGS TO PROPOUND TO YOU," SAID APOLLYON, "AND FIRST—" "IT HAD BETTER BE GOOD," MUTTERED DIABOLUS. THE OTHERS SAT AND GLOWERED.

The princes of the pit were having a council of war. Diabolus was in a cold rage born of frustration and a hate that was eating at his paunch as if to consume him. Godly-Fear had confronted him boldly, which was to be expected, for Godly-Fear had always been his most formidable foe. But that clod, Understanding! That idiot, that one-eyed numbskull—answering his most clever double-talk, with promises from Emmanuel! How dared he? Where did he find out? How? Who had got to him? And what had got into him? It was bad enough to have Godly-Fear skulking about, but to have Understanding get himself enlightened—

Diabolus crouched lower and stared at the piles of brimstone.

"The first," said Apollyon, "is this; let us withdraw ourselves from the town into the plain again. Our presence here will do us no good because—"

"Because we can't get into the castle because Godly-Fear is keeper of it," said Diabolus, chanting in a monotone like a school-boy recitation.

174

"I know, M'Lord," said Apollyon. "It is repetitious. I get tired of saying it."

"And I get tired of hearing it." Diabolus continued to stare at the brimstone. "What's your second proposition?"

"I was thinking of ambush," said Apollyon. "Our going forth from the town to draw the captains out after us—"

"It is impossible to draw them all off from the castle," said Beelzebub. "Some will lie there to keep guard. It's no use unless we can be sure that they will all come out."

"And after we get them out we can lay an ambush behind the town to rush in and take possession of the castle," Apollyon finished doggedly.

"So long as there is *one* in the town able to lift up his finger against us, Emmanuel will take their part," said Beelzebub, "and if he shall take their part, we know what time of day it will be with us."

They all looked at him to go on.

"In my judgment," he continued, "the solution is simple. Get the townsmen to sin again. In my judgment there is no way to bring them into bondage to us like inventing a way to make them sin."

"May I remind you," Diabolus said wearily, "that we have gone this route before?"

"Well, where have our doubters gotten us?" Beelzebub wanted to know. "If we'd left them at home we'd be as well off as we are now."

"My army of doubters?" roared Diabolus. "Twenty thousand handpicked—"

"Unless we could have made them the masters and governors of the castle we might as well have left them at home," Beelzebub continued. "For doubters at a distance are but like objections repelled with arguments. They have to be *in the castle.*"

"Godly-Fear is in the castle," Apollyon said quietly.

"And Captain Faith," Legion spoke for the first time.

Diabolus thought of the bold effrontery of Lord Mayor Understanding and was too furious to speak.

"Absolutely the only way to get the castle is to get the town to sin," Beelzebub said, more sure of his point now. "Let us, therefore, withdraw ourselves into the plain without expecting the captains to follow us. But before we do it, let's consult again with our trusty Diabolonians that are yet in their holds in Mansoul and set them to work to betray the town to us—"

Diabolus put his head in his hands and rocked from side to side, moaning.

"I *know* we've tried it before," said Beelzebub patiently, "but this is the way it must be done or it can't be done at all. Do you agree?"

"I am forced to agree," said Diabolus at last. "The only way to get the castle is to get the town to sin. But how? They're awake. They've had a trouncing and they seem determined not to get another one. And that miserable Captain Faith looks all too healthy. He gets healthier every day. And Understanding—" he started rocking again. "I'd give anything to throw him back in his palace and board up the windows."

"I agree with brother Beelzebub," said Legion. "And with brother Apollyon too, except for his idea of an ambush. I say withdraw our forces—"

Diabolus looked up.

"And terrify them no more," Legion went on. "No more

176

summons. No more threats. No more noisy drums. Frights awaken them and make them stand to their arms. I say leave Mansoul, lie in the field at a distance, and pretend to ignore them."

"And what then?" said Diabolus. "I don't like such nebulous strategy. What exactly is suppose to happen then?"

"Mansoul is a market town and a town that delights in commerce," said Beelzebub. "We can trade there. Send some of our Diabolonians disguised as merchants with wares to sell. Half price! What does it matter?" They were all listening avidly now. Legion warmed to his subject. "Send those who are accustomed to this work. Mr. Penny-Wise-Pound-Foolish. Mr. Sweet-World and Mr. Present-Good. They are civil and cunning. Let the Mansoulians be taken up in much business. Let them grow rich and full."

"Do you think it will work?" said Apollyon.

"I'll give you my crown to pawn if it doesn't," said Legion. "When they begin to grow full they will forget their misery. And if we are careful not to frighten them they may even fall asleep and neglect their town watch and even their castle watch. Do you see?" He turned to Diabolus.

"I'm way ahead of you," said Diabolus.

"I see," said Beelzebub. "Cumber them with abundance!"

They were taken with excitement; they all began to talk at once.

"Stuff them with goods!"

"They'll be forced to make their castle a warehouse instead of a garrison fortified against us!"

"Yes—a warehouse! Filled to the brim!"

"Then if we made a sudden assault upon them it would

be hard for the captains to take shelter there!''

"Like the parable—'the deceitfulness of riches chokes the Word!'!''

"And, 'When the heart is overcharged with surfeiting and the cares of this life—' ''

" 'All mischief comes upon them unawares'!''

"Furthermore, my lords," said Legion, "you very well know that it is not easy for a people to be filled with our things and not to have some of our Diabolonians in their homes and businesses. Where is there a Mansoulian full of this world who has not for his servants some of our own?''

"Mr. Profuse.''

"Mr. Prodigality.''

"Or some of our Diabolonian gang, as Mr. Voluptuous, Lord Opinionated, Mr. Ostentation—''

"Yessss," hissed Diabolus. "These can take the castle of Mansoul, or blow it up or make it unfit for a garrison for Emmanuel; any of these things will do.''

"Exactly," said Legion, "these, for all I know, may do it for us sooner and more thoroughly than an army of twenty thousand men.''

They all nodded agreement.

"To end as I began," said Legion, "my advice is that we quietly withdraw ourselves. No further force or forcible attempts upon the castle. At least until we've given this a try.''

They all applauded. "A veritable masterpiece of the pit,'' said Diabolus.

"Yes," said Legion. "Surfeit Mansoul's heart with the good things of this world. Full, full, full to the brim. And may the town choke on it.''

"Mansoul had better choke on it," said Diabolus. He

uncrouched himself. "Let's get our plans into action," he said briskly. "All of you. You know what you're to do." His eyes glowed red. He took out one of his cigars. He was beginning to feel like his old self again. He was in excellent spirits as the council broke up.

"I don't know what it means," thought Captain Faith as he read the letter the messenger had just handed to him. "Emmanuel will meet me in the field? What does he mean, meet me in the field?" He read it again, then thrust it into his pocket and hurried out of his lodgings and up the castle corridor. A few moments later he was knocking at the door to the suite of rooms of Lord High Secretary, in another part of the castle. He lost no time when he was admitted, but handed the Lord High Secretary the letter and said, "I don't know what he means. It's from Prince Emmanuel."

The Lord High Secretary read the note. It was a few moments before he looked up again. "The princes of the pit have had a consultation of war today," he said. "They have decided to withdraw their forces from Mansoul."

Faith was incredulous. "You mean they've given up at last?" he said.

"Don't ever make that mistake," said Lord High Secretary. "They never give up. They've given up trying to scare you, yes. At this stage you don't frighten easily. Their attempts to frighten you have only spurred you on to greater effort. You seem to thrive on trouble. No, they've just decided to leave you—"

"I do not understand."

"—to destroy yourselves."

Faith looked at the Lord High Secretary for a long moment. "How?" he said softly.

"They'll trade with you. And hope that you'll get rich. And lazy. And smug. So that you will stop watching—lower your guards. They're even hoping that you will turn this castle from a garrison into a warehouse. Fill it with worldly treasures, leave no room for your captains, your officials, your fighting men. They can wait for all this to happen. Time means nothing to them."

He looked down at the letter again. And said quickly, "Captain Faith. Are you ready for a showdown? Are you willing for a showdown?"

"M'Lord, tell me what I must do."

"This note from Emmanuel that you could not understand. It says he will meet you in the field outside Mansoul. Are you willing to take your army and meet Diabolus in the field and face him and his war lords and his army of doubters once and for all—and have it out with them?"

Captain Faith walked over to the window and stood there, looking out.

"I am speaking of a pincer movement," said Lord High Secretary. "Prince Emmanuel shall be before them and you shall be behind them, and between you both, their army shall be destroyed."

Faith looked out over the town to the plain beyond. And his eyes were wet with tears. To see his prince's face again!

He turned, saluted the Lord High Secretary. His decision was made.

"M'Lord, the battle has started. We'll prepare to go at once."

A tremendous sense of power filled the very air. Captain Faith could scarcely stand under it, and yet in some curious way he felt that he could soar. The Lord High Secretary gave him a briefing and his orders and a special battle cry and bade him farewell.

"Remember," he said, as Faith left, "you will not be fighting alone."

Did they want to fight? Oh, *did they want to fight!* When Captain Faith made the declaration of war known to the officers and elders, there wasn't one of them who wanted to miss the battle! To see their beloved prince again! To have another chance to show him they loved him—that they meant business! Hallelujah—what mercy—what a master!

"The king's trumpeters!" Captain Faith ordered.

"In the market square?" they wanted to know.

"Market square? No!" cried Faith. "Climb up to the castle battlements. Blow as you've never blown before! Make the best music that heart can invent!" They climbed to the very battlements and blew as if they were determined to reach Shaddai himself. It stopped Diabolus in his tracks.

"Listen." He motioned his band of war lords quiet. "Is it—no, it isn't Boot-and-saddle. It isn't Horse-and-away. And it isn't Charge! It's just plain joy! What do these mad men have to be so merry and glad about?"

Nobody answered him. "I *hate* joy!" he bellowed.

They listened a moment. Then it struck him. "It can mean only one thing," he said incredulous, "Prince Emmanuel is actually coming to their aid!"

He moved so fast he gave the illusion of springing in three directions at once. "We must get out of here. Now. Out to the plains. We can fight better out there."

"But sire," they began, "with Prince Emmanuel coming—"

"All right!" he shrieked, "if we can't fight, we can run!"

It was a busy night.

Diabolus and his army retreated to the plains outside Mansoul. Captain Faith got his army ready for battle. He gave his men their orders and the battle cry. He told them they would see their prince in the field next day and it was like pouring oil on a fire. The excitement spread throughout the town. There wasn't one warrior, great or small, who didn't want to go!

At last they were ready to march. Captain Faith gave last minute orders, the trumpeters sounded the call to march, and they were off! They were on the offensive now—to outflank, to surround, to destroy, to fight to the finish! And their battle cry was "The sword of Prince Emmanuel and the shield of Captain Faith!" which is, being interpreted, "The Word and faith."

Captain Experience discovered they'd started without him because he'd been so badly wounded, but he couldn't stay out of it. He called for his crutches and flew along on them as though they'd been seven-league boots!

The Diabolonians saw them coming, braced themselves for the fight. But what *was* this? What spirit possessed these Mansoulians? They were no longer timid, easy to frighten. They were coming on crutches, in bandages, in slings, in wheelchairs—as if nothing could hold them back! On, on, they were coming, crying, "The sword of Prince Emmanuel and the shield of Captain Faith."

Diabolus watched them coming. There was nothing to do but fall upon them with all his deadly force. He shouted orders and the battle was joined. But almost immediately they began to outflank him, wielding that "two-edged sword," fighting as if inspired, with a strength that belied their seedy appearance. His doubters were dropping at an alarming rate. Some of the key Mansoulians had to be knocked out of the battle, and soon. He wet his lips, drew in his paunch, and peered through the dust.

Then he saw Willbewill.

In a flash he saw a montage of Wills. Will who had faced him from the city wall when he took the form of a dragon. Cocksure Will crying that day in his office, "I am the master of my fate!" Foolish Will, heady with power, resisting Shaddai. Limping broken Will, yielding to Emmanuel. Gullible Will, kowtowing to Carnal-Security. Battered Will, doggedly apprehending Diabolonians long after the battle was lost. And now this Will coming toward him and his bodyguards through the battle dust, revived and determined. But not cocky.

"I would prefer him cocky," thought Diabolus, bracing himself, "but let's have a go at it."

In the second before they clashed Diabolus saw that Will had someone by his side.

It was Captain Faith.

# DEFEAT OF THE DIABOLONIANS

ILL LEAPED THROUGH THE AIR AND LANDED ON TWO SALVATION-DOUBT-ERS, KNOCKING THEM TO THE GROUND AND RUNNING THEM THROUGH WITH his sword. Then he sprang back and took on all comers and his blows were like the blows of a giant. The doubters hit the dust before him as he cut and battered shrewdly, with deadly accuracy. Faith leapt upon them too, helping Will put them into disorder. But as one doubter fell, three more sprang to take his place, for Diabolus had surrounded himself with protection.

A few feet away, Captain Good-Hope fell upon the Vocation-Doubters, and they were sturdy men but he slashed them to bits.

The plain was alive with fighting now. This was a do-or-die battle. Everyone sensed it, from Captain Faith down to the weakest Mansoulian. And from Diabolus and his war lords down to the puniest and meanest doubter.

Everyone was in it. The doubters were in an uproar. Swords were flashing in the sun, and slings were coming from the distant castle battlements too, for Lord High Secretary was far from idle. He had commanded that the slings from the castle should be played, and his men could aim their ammunition to shave the hair off a doubter or slice him up, with equal ease.

The battle raged on—each side advancing and retreating in turn. Each time the Mansoulian army was forced to retreat, it would rally and come back for more with the battle cry—"The sword of Emmanuel and the shield of Captain Faith!"

But as the day wore on and the battle waxed hotter, the weariness came, and finally, utter confusion. Slings. Arrows. Shouts of victory. Captain Torment. Admonitions of courage. Whispers. Perseverance-Doubters. Swords flashing. Joy-Doubters. Lord Willbewill is wounded. It's his leg, only his leg. Captain Insatiable. Slings from the castle. Retreat, retreat, just a little, give some ground. Faith, Faith! Where is Captain Faith? Moans of pain. Willbewill. Just a scratch. It's his bad leg. He was already limping with that leg anyhow. Another wound won't matter. Dust and smoke. Rest a bit. Patch up the wounded. Give them first-aid. Grace-Doubters. Swords flashing. He would gladly lose his leg to see his prince again. The din is terrible. Salvation-Doubters. Advance, advance, quit yourselves like men of valor. Emmanuel hasn't come yet. Captain Rage. Slings from the castle. Perhaps Shaddai is dead. The gates are broken, the gates are broken, the walls are cracked, the streets are dirty, the lights are damaged. A valiant army in the field this day. Mr. Conscience is wounded. You have shown yourselves men of courage, you have answered the challenge, you have come on crutches, you have come in wheelchairs, you were weak and wounded before the battle even started. Mr. Corruption. Oh, our captains are a motley crew, a motley crew, a motley crew. Glory-Doubters. Lord Understanding can't see too well. It is too late, we've gone too far, we are wounded, we are weak. *Who have we but thee, Emmanuel? There is none beside thee.* Go into the fight again. Captain Fury. It's the showdown, it's the showdown, go into the fight again. O Mansoul dear, your strength is gone, your strength is gone, your strength is gone. Go into the fight again. Go into the fight again. Go into the fight again. No. There is a retreat on both sides. There's a respite. Don't fight any more. Don't fight any more. Don't fight any more. What did Captain Faith say, we can't hear him, we can't hear him, what did he say?

Be still.

What does Captain Faith say?

"Gentlemen!" cried Faith through the confusion. "Soldiers, and my brothers in this design, I rejoice to see in the field for our prince this day so stout and so valiant an army and such faithful lovers of Mansoul!"

Be still.

"You have shown yourselves men of courage against the Diabolonian forces; so that, for all their boasting—"

Still, still.

"—for all their boasting they have not yet much cause to boast of their gettings. Now take the courage you want, it is yours for the taking, and get yourselves back into the fight. For we must make this second assault upon Diabolus. And in a few minutes after the next engagement, this time, you shall see your prince show himself in the field!"

Even as he spoke, a messenger handed him a message. He read it quickly and shouted, "Emmanuel is even now on his way!"

Oh the roar that went up! "Praise be to Shaddai who giveth us the victory!" It made the Diabolonians tremble. Like men raised from the dead, the Mansoulians got ready to charge again. They rose, they advanced, they charged, they spread out, they cried, "The sword of Prince Emmanuel and the shield of Captain Faith!"

And then—the sound of distant trumpets! And in the heat of the battle, through the smoke and dust, Captain Faith lifted his eyes and saw Prince Emmanuel coming with colors flying, trumpets sounding, the feet of his men scarcely touching the ground! Diabolus and his war lords saw it too and fled in panic, forsaking their army, leaving them to fall. Faith gave the orders, the Mansoulian army disengaged itself and retreated toward the walls of the town, leaving Diabolus' army the field. Then—the giant pincer movement! Prince Emmanuel on one side, Faith on the other, the Diabolonians in the middle, squeezed, crushed, smothered. And the two great armies fought their way, slashed their way, prayed their way toward each other until they met there on the plain, the enemy trampled underneath.

And the cry went up again, "The sword of Prince Emmanuel and the shield of Captain Faith!" And the ground fairly split with the noise of it.

Diabolus and his war lords looked back from a distance. Their army of twenty thousand doubters with their captains and officers, and an undetermined number of Diabolonians that had lived in Mansoul were sprawled in ignominious defeat. From the looks of it, few had escaped; there was no way of telling at the moment. They were spread like dung upon the earth.

A shadow sped along the ground in front of the little group, wings outspread, moving swiftly toward the battlefield. Diabolus watched it for a moment. Then he looked up.

It was a vulture.

# TRIUMPHAL RETURN FROM THE FIELD

R. PRYWELL STOOD ON A PLATFORM ALONG THE MAIN STREET OF MANSOUL, AND LOOKED OUT OVER THE CROWDS. THE PLATFORM HAD BEEN HASTILY erected but the rough work was covered with boughs and sweet-smelling moss and the railing was entwined with flowers and vines of every description. There were other platforms like it all along the way, and above them the balconies on the houses had been made into veritable gardens with vines streaming down, and almost reaching the crowds in the streets. The din of shouting was deafening, as the Mansoulians jostled and jockeyed for vantage positions and ran to and fro with flowers in garlands and chains and bouquets. Everyone, it seemed, had flowers of one sort or another and the air was redolent with a sweet perfume.

Outside on the plain the dust of battle had settled. The captains and elders and gentry of Mansoul had saluted Emmanuel in the field and welcomed him with a thousand welcomes. And he had smiled upon them and said, "Peace be to you." They had put their camps in order and now they were all returning in a triumphal march.

The sun was shining now; it was like a glorious morning after a fearful night. It would be impossible to describe their joy, Prywell thought.

Then, through the din he heard the music. They must be drawing near the gates. He could hear the choirs singing. Wait. Listen. He tried to catch what they were singing. Oh yes, "Lift up your heads, oh ye gates; and be ye lifted up, ye everlasting doors; and the King of Glory shall come in!" He strained his ears to catch it. Ah—just a moment. Oh yes. Another choir now. "Who is this King of Glory—" He caught it now—"The Lord strong and mighty; the Lord mighty in battle!" They came out in full voice then, and choir answered choir as the song progressed and repeated itself. How they sing, thought Prywell, as though they'd burst their throats. Now the music could be heard above the din as, one by one, the Mansoulians stopped shouting to listen.

Now there were trumpets and songs all along the thoroughfare, coming closer—"They have seen thy goings, O God; even the goings of my God, my King, in the sanctuary!" Before the crowd could hardly take this in, the first of the procession was in sight. Singers—players on instruments—timbrels—

"Blessed be the prince that cometh in the name of his father, Shaddai!"

Someone shouted it and the crowd took it up. "Blessed be he that cometh in the name of the Lord!"

"Yea—Captain Faith!" It was a new shout, up the way. Prywell strained his eyes to see. Yes—the captains were coming now!

"Faith!" Prywell found himself shouting along with the rest, as the captain went by. Then the others—Captain Good-Hope, Captain Love, Captain Guileless, Captain Patience, each with his officers and soldiers, banners streaming.

"Yea—Captain Experience!" Yes, the Mansoulian captains and officers were there, too. Mr. Knowledge was there, Mr. Mind, all of them. Prywell saluted them as they went by.

They were battered and bandaged but their faces were shining. And then—

"THE PRINCE!"

The cry split the air. And banners waved and flowers were thrown upon the street by the crowds in the balconies—garlands of flowers and chains of flowers and bouquets of flowers and single flowers of every kind—until the street was a blanket of flowers and the perfume lifted to the sky. The prince was coming! The prince was coming!

And then, in the crowds, everything stopped.

The people in the balconies and the people on the streets stopped and the waving stopped and the shouting stopped and the streamers in the air floated to the ground and stopped and the children who were running stopped.

And all that could be heard was the muted clatter of horses' hoofs on the flowers and the muted rumbling of the wheels of Emmanuel's chariot on the flowers. And the cry from the hearts of the people, unspoken and unheard, hung in the air like a silent anthem.

The pillars of the prince's chariot were of silver, the botttom of it was gold and the covering of it was of purple. And the prince's armor was of beaten gold. And when they saw him, the townfolk wept silently, astonished at his love for them.

And so he rode by.

Prywell watched through his tears until the chariot was out of sight, on its way to the castle, where Lord Mayor Understanding, and Lord Willbewill and Mr. Conscience and all the gentry of the place were waiting. There would be no shouts, no speeches. They would bow before him and kiss the dust at his feet. And they would bless him and praise him and thank him for pitying them in their misery and returning to them with mercies. And then he would go into the castle, which had been cleaned and prepared for him by the presence of the Lord High Secretary and the work of Captain Faith.

Prywell climbed down from the platform and mingled with the crowds in the street. They were closing in behind the rear guard of Emmanuel's chariot. And as he trod through the flowers he remembered the nights he had prowled the streets, huddled against the chill wind and kicking the rubbish aside, until he had found Mr. Mischief.

# LINGERING CULPRITS

R. PRYWELL SAT IN HIS STUDY AND FLIPPED THROUGH THE PAPERS ON HIS DESK. HE READ AGAIN THE NOTICES THAT HAD BEEN POSTED IN THE MARKET SQUARE.

## MANDATE

### FROM PRINCE EMMANUEL
### TO THE TOWN OF MANSOUL

*Weep not, but go your way, eat the fat, and drink the sweet, and send portions to them for whom nothing is prepared; for the joy of your Lord is your strength. I am returned to Mansoul with mercies, and my name shall be set up, exalted and magnified by it.*

## MANDATE

### FROM LORD MAYOR UNDERSTANDING
### TO THE TOWN OF MANSOUL

*An order has been given by the blessed Prince Emmanuel that the townsmen should, without further delay, appoint some to go forth into the plain to bury the dead that are there—the dead that fell by the sword of Emmanuel and by the shield of Captain Faith, that the remembrance of the name and being of those enemies might be cut off from the thought of the town of Mansoul.*

*Mr. Godly-Fear and Mr. Upright have been appointed to be overseers in this matter, and persons are to be put under them to work in the fields, to bury the slain that lie dead upon the plains.*

*These are their places of employment: Some will make the graves; some will bury the dead, along with their arms, their colors, their banners; and some will go to and fro in the plains and also round about the borders of Mansoul to see if any skull, or a bone, or a piece of a bone of a doubter is yet to be found above ground anywhere near the town. If any are found, it is ordered that the searchers should set up a mark or a sign thereby, that those appointed to bury them might find them and bury them out of sight; that the name and remembrance of any Diabolonian doubter might be blotted out from under heaven; and that the children, and they that are to be born in Mansoul, might not know, if possible, what a skull, what a bone, or a piece of a bone of a doubter was.*

*By order of*

*LORD MAYOR UNDERSTANDING*

Yes, Emmanuel had come home. The garments of the people of Mansoul had been mended and washed. The enemy dead had been buried. There was music and rejoicing throughout the whole town of Mansoul because their prince had again granted to them his presence and the light of his countenance. The sun shone and God's peace again filled the air like a sweet perfume. The long long struggle was over at last.

But Mr. Prywell knew better.

Or, more to the point, he knew the major struggle was over—the ravaging war, the horror of the dark nights, the sickness, the loneliness, the despair, the hopeless defeat. But the whole of it was not over. Skirmishes were still to come, and always would.

He turned up some memos, an accumulation of the past week, and read them over.

## MEMO

From the office of
LORD MAYOR UNDERSTANDING

*Dear Will:*

*Everywhere I turn I hear that you are more of a menace to the remaining lurking Diabolonians than ever before. It's a pity that some of them escaped with life and limb from the hand of their suppressors and got back to their miserable dens and cracks, but from the way you are pursuing them night and day I have no fear that we shall keep ahead of them. Of course you know that the town of Mansoul seeks their complete destruction, as they are an abomination to us.*

*There's a chap I'm sending to you shortly to help you in this work and you may get a bit of a shock when you see him. He's a fellow by the name of Self-Denial, and he bears many a scar to show for it. Overlook his appearance; he's pretty dog-eared, but his scars are scars of honor.*

*Thank you, Will, and keep up the good work. Keep in touch.*
*UNDERSTANDING.*

## MEMO

From the office of
LORD WILLBEWILL

*Dear Understanding:*

*Keep in touch? No fear of that! I shall keep in close touch with you, not only because I enjoy your fellowship but because I need your enlightenment, and I know your enlightenment comes from the Lord High Secretary. Every time I come away from a session with you I am encouraged and fortified and go back into the fray with a keener insight. I know what I'm fighting and why, and am not so apt to go off on tangential sprees, railing at inconsequentials while the real business at hand is right under my nose. How I thank Shaddai that old Prejudice is slain and I do not have to hunt for him! And I thank Shaddai that you are in your office studying daily; I count on this. I think you are even developing a sense of humor.*

*WILL.*

*PS: You should thank Mr. Conscience, not me. Now that the old duffer is out of his wheelchair and off crutches, he bellows about more than ever. I used to think him a pesky nuisance, but now I love him, even when he roars. See you in the castle in the morning.*

*W.*

# MEMO

❖ ◆ ❖

### From the office of
### LORD MAYOR UNDERSTANDING

*Dear Conscience:*

*I do not need to ask if you are well, for your roaring can sometimes be heard clear up to my office. I am not complaining though, for it means you are tender, and the more tender you are, the more noise you make. Be sure to keep in touch with me, so you can roar at the proper times—though I know your real enlightenment comes from the Lord High Secretary, bless his name! Keep close to him, dear Conscience, and roar away. We might not always like you for it, but even when you have indigestion and rumble, we tremble! See you at the castle in the morning.*

*UNDERSTANDING.*

# MEMO

❖ ◆ ❖

### From the office of
### MR. CONSCIENCE

*Dear Understanding:*

*I don't have time to answer your note. I am too busy roaring. My hide is so tender that the mere whiff of a Diabolonian slinking out of his hold is enough to jar me to the core, and I dash off a memo to Will, who is usually already out pouncing on another one.*

*You are right; I am immediately responsible to the Lord High Secretary, but so are we all. Emmanuel has decreed that we all work together under him.*

*As you know, I am in fine fettle, and getting about nicely without the wheelchair or even a crutch. And no more sleeping pills. See you at the castle in the morning.*

CONSCIENCE.

## MEMO

From the office of
LORD WILLBEWILL

*Dear Conscience:*

*Your memos are piling up; there were three when I got back from my rounds tonight. Sometimes I thank Shaddai that the Diabolonians still lurking here are unimportant ones; then I have a session in the castle along with you and Understanding, and listen to Prince Emmanuel and the Lord High Secretary, and go away knowing again that there is no harmless Diabolonian. How I thank Shaddai for you all! Keep the memos coming.*

WILL.

## MEMO

From the office of
MR. CONSCIENCE

*Dear Will:*

*You make me sound like a tyrant. I roar. You jump. Do you want me to stop bothering you?*

CONSCIENCE.

# MEMO

From the office of
LORD WILLBEWILL

*Dear Conscience:*
*I told you to keep the memos coming. What would we do without*
*you? See you at the castle in the morning.*

*WILL.*

Prywell put the memos down and looked out his window, across the town. Yes, the skirmishes would go on, but under conditions of calm determination and joy. It would be a joy tempered with caution and born of the knowledge that Mansoul could never stand without complete dependence upon Emmanuel, born of the admonition: ''Let him that thinketh he standeth take heed, lest he fall.'' Born of wisdom.

He glanced back at the papers on his desk. Vigilance, he thought, was the key word. The never-ending watching. From the highest officials down to the humblest Mansoulian. Vigilance.

He picked up a detailed report—Case #86736A: THE CASE OF THE DOUBTING DIABOLONIANS—that had just come in that morning. It was from the Mansoul Bureau of Investigation. To a great extent the warfare now involved the behind-the-scenes activities of this great network of hand-picked secret investigators. He had already read the report, but he read it again to stow it away in his mind before he put it in the files.

It had begun one starless night, just outside the Ear-gate.

A figure was crouched there, waiting. Another figure emerged through the shadows, walked past, paused, came back, crouched beside the first. They were silent for a while; then the first one asked a question and they began their conversation.

"Looking for someone?"

"Yes."

"Who?"

"For Mr. Evil-Questioning."

"Who sent you?"

"Diabolus."

"What is the password?"

"Get 'em to doubt."

"All right. Follow me."

"I have three others with me."

"Where are they?"

"Crouched behind the rocks—over there."

"Tell them to follow you, keeping a few yards behind. Understand?"

"I understand."

The strange procession began: the two figures ahead, the others following, paced well behind. They entered at Eargate and proceeded up the dark streets, ducking into the shadows, running past the streetlights, keeping in the back streets and alleys until they finally came to a lonely house well back from the road, all in darkness. They went up to the door. There was a stealthy knock in code—one-two-three—one, by the one who had led them in; then a voice from within.

"Who's there?"

"Get 'em to doubt."

And the door opened and disclosed a surprisingly rotund and healthy creature, bland and smiling. He stretched out his arms.

"And whom have we here?" he asked heartily.

"Doubters. Three of them," said the first creature, and slithered away into the shadows.

"Come in quickly," said the resident, their host. "Did anyone see you?" Without waiting for an answer he drew them in and closed the door.

"And which doubters are you?" he began, as he beckoned them into the room and went over to light a stubby candle. "Let me have a look at you."

"Faith-Doubter," said one.

"Faith-Doubter! Well, now. I've been waiting and hoping for you." He shushed the others. "No matter who you are. A doubt is a doubt, I always say. And I'm delighted to see you. Are you all from the same town?"

"No, we are from different towns," they all began at once, but he interrupted.

"No matter, no matter," he chortled happily, "from different places, or all the same, I can see at once that at heart you are all town boys. A doubter is a doubter, I always say, and welcome to the town of Mansoul. I can use you, no matter where you're from or who you are. Delighted, delighted. Any little doubt will do. Yes, indeed. Any little doubt at all."

He busied himself over a stove and stirred a pot that was steaming with foul odors and finally emerged triumphant with three bowls of brew. "You need a bit of nourishment," he said, handing them the brew. They fell upon it at once, talking between slurps, telling him who they were and why they'd come and thanking him all the while for giving them shelter.

"I can see you are starved," he said fondly.

"We are," they said. "Our paunches are empty, always—"

"You must speak softly," he hissed.

"—always growling for the inhabitants of Mansoul," they went on in whispers. "But, thanks be to Shaddai, the pickings are slim."

"Ah yes," the host said sadly, "the pickings are slim, for Mansoul is on alert, but never fear, I am always on the alert too."

This thought picked him up considerably; he began to beam again. "I have an alias of course, for the benefit of the town—we do have to be so careful, but my name as you well know—"

There was a loud pounding at the door. And immediately shouts.

"Open up in the name of the king!"

They sat stunned for a moment; then their host rallied. "I'll have to let them in," he said, "but I'll talk us out of it. You get into that closet, and quickly!"

He ushered them to the closet and pushed them in. "Quick quick quick quick quick," he whispered, half commanding, half assuring. "Now away with you. Everything's going to be all right. I'll see to that." And he turned and went to the door, lifted the latch, opened it a crack, his countenance beaming with innocent surprise.

"Yes, gentlemen?" he said to the officers outside. Their leader came right to the point. "You are under arrest. You are Mr. Evil-Questioning?"

"There must be some mistake. My name is Mr. Honest-Inquiry." He tried to exert his weight against the door but they pushed it open and entered, filling the room with their formidable presence, their glances darting about.

He tried again. "I simply inquire into the word of Shaddai and Emmanuel—"

"You rob Shaddai of his glory. You rob Emmanuel of the sufficiency of his undertaking. You despise the work of the Lord High Secretary. And as long as you smuggle in doubters you rob Mansoul of its strength and keep it from appropriating all the promises of Shaddai."

"But my name is simply Mr. Honest-Inquiry—"

"Your name is Evil-Questioning, you're smuggling doubters, and you are wanted in the name of the king."

"Doubters? What doubters? Sir, I beg of you, you have made a ghastly mistake—"

But the other officers were already dragging the doubters from the closet. Mr. Evil-Questioning turned to his captor. "And who might you be, my good man?"

"Diligence of the death squad. Inspector Diligence to you, serving under the authority of Lord Willbewill." He glanced at his men, jerked his head toward the door, and they began to drag the doubters out.

"But sir," began Evil-Questioning, "don't take these good men away. They are only honest doubters that I have harbored out of pity—"

"Then you can come along too," said Inspector Diligence, "and explain it all to Emmanuel."

At this, Evil-Questioning sank to the floor. "No—" he cried. "I can operate here in quiet and secrecy and eke out a living, but to make me face Emmanuel—I pray you—" He

203

began to whimper now. "I shall die, I shall die—"

Inspector Diligence turned to his men. "Take him away," he said.

Prywell put the report down. They were all tried, got the extreme penalty, and the case was closed.

He rummaged through the rest of the case histories that had accumulated on his desk, ready for filing, Mr. Let-Good-Slip. Apprehended one day as he was busy in the market.

Mr. Clip-Promise. He was made a public example, for by his doings much of the king's coin was abused. He was arraigned and sentenced to be whipped before he was executed. Pretty severe, but honest traders in Mansoul were sensible of the great abuse that one clipper of promises, in little time, may do to the town.

Mr. Self-Love. Apprehended and committed to custody; but there were so many that were allied to him in Mansoul, his judgment was deferred. But at last Mr. Self-Denial had stood up and said: "If such villains as these may be winked at in Mansoul, I will lay down my commission." So Self-Love was banished, but some in Mansoul muttered at it.

Then there were Mr. No-Love, Mr. Mistrust, Mr. Sloth, Mr. Live-by-Feeling, Mr. Legal-Life.

Here was a strange case, thought Prywell. Mr. Carnal-Sense. The Case of the Elusive Ghost. He'd been captured, more than once. But he'd always managed to escape mysteriously, to lurk in the Diabolonian dens by day and haunt, like a ghost, honest men's houses by night. There was a reward out for his capture; the proclamation in the market square said that whoever could discover Carnal-Sense and apprehend him and slay him should be made keeper of the treasury of Mansoul. Many tried to capture him, for this reward was quite an inducement. But though he was often discovered, no one could bring him in to stay.

And that old nimble jack, Unbelief. Prywell thought of his file, which was now bulging, and sighed. He was unquestionably out on the plains somewhere, or in Diabolus' den, masterminding the undercover syndicate in Mansoul. And he'd be around nibbling at little things, fussing and quibbling and questioning right up to the time Mansoul left the kingdom of Universe to go to dwell with Shaddai. If Mansoul had it all to do over, thought Prywell, the answer would be so simple: just believe Shaddai.

Prywell stacked the reports and pushed them to the side of his desk. No, he thought, some of the cases might never be closed. There would always be some Diabolonians in Mansoul, cropping up, smuggled in, their ways subtle, their disguises clever. Emmanuel was allowing them to stay.

At the thought of Emmanuel, Prywell started, looked at his timepiece, and bolted for the door. Emmanuel was speaking to the townspeople in the market square. If Prywell did not get going, he'd be late. He hurried down the street.

# EMMANUEL'S EXPLANATION

"ES, I SUFFER DIABOLONIANS TO DWELL IN YOUR WALLS, O MANSOUL; IT IS TO KEEP THEE WATCHFUL, TO TRY THY LOVE," EMMANUEL WAS SAYING AS Prywell entered the market square. He found himself a place at the edge of the crowd and listened. It was as though Emmanuel had read his thoughts—as if a conversation that had begun in his study was continuing in the market square.

"It is to cause you to prize my noble captains and their soldiers. It is to cause you to prize my mercy. And it is also that you be made to remember the deplorable condition you once were in," Emmanuel went on. "O my Mansoul, should I slay all them within, many there be without that would bring you into bondage. Were all those within cut off, those without would find you sleeping. Then, as in a moment, they would swallow up my Mansoul. Therefore I left them within your walls not to do you hurt but to do you good, the which they must, if you watch and fight against them. Know therefore that whatever they shall tempt you to, my design is that they should drive you, not farther off, but nearer to my father, to teach you war, to make petitioning desirable to you.

"Show me, then, your love, my Mansoul, and let not those that are within your walls take your affections away from him that has redeemed your soul. Yea, let the sight of a Diabolonian heighten your love to me.

"Someday I shall take you to my father's kingdom, where you shall no more hear the evil-tidings or the noise of the Diabolonian drum.

"There, O Mansoul, you shall meet with many of those that have been like you, and that have been partakers of your sorrows; even such as I have chosen and redeemed and set apart, as you, for my father's court and city-royal. All they will be glad in you, and you, when you see them, shall be glad in your heart.

"There are things, O Mansoul, even things of my father's providing, and mine, that never were seen since the beginning of the world. They are laid up with my father and sealed up among his treasures for you, until you come to his kingdom to enjoy them.

"And there, in that kingdom are those that rejoice in you now; but how much more, when they shall see you exalted to honor! My father will then send them for you to fetch you. And you, O my Mansoul, shall ride upon the wings of the wind!

"I have loved you, Mansoul. I bought you for a price; a price not of corruptible things, as of silver and gold, but a price of blood, my own blood, which I spilled freely to make you mine, and to reconcile you to my father.

"And I stood by you in your backsliding, when you were

unfaithful, though you did not know I was there. It was I who made your way dark and bitter. It was I who put Mr. Godly-Fear to work. It was I who stirred up Conscience and Understanding and Will. It was I who made you seek me, and in finding me, find your own health and happiness.

"Nothing can hurt you but sin; nothing can grieve me but sin; nothing can make you fall before your foes but sin; beware of sin, my Mansoul.

"I have taught you to watch, to fight, to pray, and to make war against your foes; so now I command you to believe that my love is *constant* to you.

"O my Mansoul, how I have set my heart, my love upon you!

"Show me your love—and hold fast—until I take you to my father's kingdom where there is no more sorrow, no grief, no pain . . . .

"Where you shall never be afraid again . . . ."

It was a long time before the crowd in the market square broke up. Emmanuel had addressed them from his chariot, and they waited in respect and worship until his captains had escorted him out of the square and back to the castle.

Will and Understanding and Conscience turned with the others to return to their homes.

"So the Diabolonians will always be with us," said Will. "Is there no end to the battle?"

"He has promised no end to the battle as long as we are here," said Understanding. "But as he said, it's to keep us watchful. We're not in Shaddai's country yet."

Will did not answer; Understanding went on. "Does that make you discouraged?"

"I suppose I shall get weary in well-doing sometimes," Will admitted, "and the landscape of Mansoul will look bleak. But right now I'm not discouraged. I think it's more of an awesome sense of responsibility. In this triumvirate, I am the culprit. Or I could be. I make the choices. And I could ignore you even though you enlighten me. Or you, Conscience, even though you roar."

"Our responsibility is just as great," said Understanding. "If we mislead you, you could, in all good faith, make the wrong choices."

"Then none of us is of any use without the other," said Conscience.

"No," said Understanding, "and none of us is of any use without King Shaddai and Prince Emmanuel and the Lord High Secretary. Take out any part and Mansoul falls into a shambles. Left to ourselves we can do nothing but fail."

The crowd jostled them but they went on talking as if they were alone in the Universe.

"Is this way better than the freedom you had before?" said Understanding, though he knew the answer.

"The freedom we had before was like—" Will struggled for words, "like birds flying through broken windows in-and-out of a deserted house—flying aimlessly, going nowhere."

"Do you love him because you have to?" Understanding's probing was gentle; their talk was to reiterate their faith, and in their talking they strengthened each other.

"I do not have to love him," said Will. "I am free. He has always left me free to do as I please."

"Then?"

"I love him because I want to," Will said simply. "And I can never love him enough."

By this time they were at the edge of the square.

But, Mr. Prywell was already over on the other side of the town, prowling through the streets.